EDMUND CAMPION

EDMUND CAMPION
HERO OF GOD'S
UNDERGROUND

Written by Harold C. Gardiner, S.J.

Illustrated by Rose Goudket

IGNATIUS PRESS   SAN FRANCISCO

Cover design by Riz Boncan Marsella
Cover illustration by Christopher J. Pelicano

With ecclesiastical approval
Published by Ignatius Press, San Francisco, 1992
All rights reserved
ISBN 0–89870–387–5
Library of Congress catalogue number 91–76073
Printed in the United States of America

CONTENTS

AUTHOR'S NOTE

The most complete life of Saint Edmund in English is the one by Richard Simpson, written in 1866. (I have used the edition of 1907, London, Burns and Oates.) Waugh relied heavily on it when he wrote his exquisite study of Campion in 1935 (Sheed & Ward). These two lives have furnished the factual basis for the present work. In addition, I have made use of *Records of the English Province of the Society of Jesus* by Henry Foley, S.J. (London: Manresa Press, 1875 ff.) and have consulted such works as Philip Hughes' *The Reformation in England*, especially vol. III, "Religio Depopulata" (New York: Macmillan, 1954).

The characters here depicted are all actual historical figures, with the exception of some minor ones.

Most of Father Campion's longer speeches, as when he addresses his captors or defends himself at the trial, are in his own words as preserved in official documents. I have modernized these as little as possible and only in order to make them more intelligible to young readers of the twentieth century.

I have used several devices which rest on probability. Young William Harrington, for example, did meet Father Campion at Mount Saint John in Yorkshire. Since Catholic families under the persecution would naturally come to know one another, it is likely that William was at the home of the Yates during the search and capture. There is no historical evidence for this coincidence. Young William and John Yate could well have been friends, though there is no record of it. Again, William's presence at the execution is also a convenient device, though it is possible he was present.

In all fairness, it ought to be said that many priests and laymen who were captured with Saint Edmund, or imprisoned in the Tower with him, have been passed over in this account. Fathers Ford and Collington, for example, who were captured with Saint Edmund at Lyford Grange, suffered long imprisonment for the Faith. And Ralph Sherwin and Alexander Briant, both admitted to the Society of Jesus before their death, also met martyrs' deaths along with Saint Edmund.

Many brave laymen suffered the same fate, but this has been an attempt to tell the story of Saint Edmund alone. He is, in a very true sense, the prototype and the forerunner of all those priests, religious, and laymen, who, for the next 150 years, would water the Faith in England with their blood.

The great boost given to Catholic life and Catholic resistance by the missionary work of Fathers Campion and Persons is well sketched in Hughes' *The Reformation in England*, vol. III, pages 306 ff. Here is a brief passage:

It is a familiar story how the two great missionaries [Persons and Campion] fared, and how, after a rarely active thirteen months, the one was taken and the other forced out by a chase so hot that he did not dare expose any Catholic home to the risk of giving him shelter. And what the two actually accomplished . . . has set their memory in a light that nearly four hundred years has not dimmed. What exactly was it that was special to their effort? . . .

In the apostolate of Persons and Campion, we have, for once, the spectacle of the right idea brilliantly carried out: understanding of the first need, namely, to know the position exactly; the organised, rapid tour, next, to survey the whole country; the "national mission" by two preachers of genius which this becomes; a work of reconciliations by conversions over an area so extensive, and covered so speedily, that the two Jesuits seem simultaneously everywhere; a work whose kind and whose effects cannot be kept secret—all the Catholics of England, it seems, knew of it, half expected (we feel) to meet the famous priests sooner or later; and they knew, of course, as did all England, of the elaborate hunt to capture them.

One further note should be added. George Eliot was indeed the man who tracked Saint Edmund down, but I have telescoped history. It is not known that Eliot was on the track of Saint Edmund as early as I have made out in the story. Again, it is not clear whether Eliot was under the direct supervision of Lord Leicester or Lord Burleigh. Sir Francis Walsingham, who had charge of most of the secret police, may have directed Eliot's search.

The episode about the "Last Will and Testament of John Shakespeare" is another of the historical probabilities for which there seems to be very good justification. The most extended treatment of this intriguing speculation is contained in *Shakespeare Rediscovered*, by Clara Longworth de Chambrun (New York and London: Charles Scribner's Sons, 1938), chapter 4, "The Spiritual Testament of John Shakespeare", pages 64–80, 303–9.

Those who would like to follow the fate of the Jesuits in England after the death of Saint Edmund would do well to read *The Autobiography of a Hunted Priest*, the retranslated diary of Father John Gerard, edited by Reverend Philip Caraman, S.J. (New York: Farrer, Straus and Cudahy, 1952); and *An Autobiography from the Jesuit Underground*, the diary of Reverend John Weston, S.J. (same editor and publisher, 1954). The adventures of these two priests took place some fifty years after the death of Saint Edmund.

Their stories illustrate the spirit of heroism that so caught the imagination of England and the world through the short apostolic life and martyr's death of Saint Edmund Campion, S.J., "the man who bragged the best".

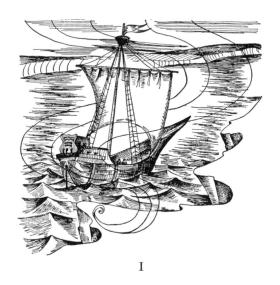

I

THE JEWEL MERCHANT COMES
BACK HOME

THE EARLY DAWN was just beginning to whiten still more the white cliffs of Dover when the little channel boat nosed its way into the harbor. Early-morning mists were swirling and lifting around the jetty that ran out into the harbor, so that the two men standing in the prow of the boat had difficulty making out the land.

But they kept peering and searching, and anyone watching them would have seen in their attitude a certain wariness, a certain caution. What were they looking for; what were they on guard against? They were, obviously, just two Englishmen coming back from the Continent. They had sailed from the French port of Calais on the evening of June 24, 1579. One of the Englishmen was dressed like a wealthy merchant; the other was clearly his servant.

"Things don't seem to have changed much, Ralph", said the merchant. The sails flapped idly as the ship made its way to the landing steps. "It's been a good while since I left this port, and though things have gone sorely for so many of our dear countrymen, one would not think, from this peaceful scene, that so much cruelty and danger stalk abroad in the fair land of England."

"No, Father", began Ralph, but his companion broke in almost roughly.

"Hush, Ralph, man; have you so soon forgotten our lessons and our practice sessions? I am *not* Father; I'm *Mr*. Edmunds. And you are *not* Brother Ralph, but *my man* Ralph. It will be hard to remember, after we have lived together in the Society of Jesus and have been such good brothers in Christ, but we run the risk of betraying one another and the cause if we don't keep up the roles we have taken on."

He threw an arm affectionately around Ralph's shoulder and went on: "I don't like it all any more than you do, Ralph, but I have no doubt that in this peaceful-looking little harbor the spies are already lying in wait for us. One false slip and we will find ourselves straightway clapped into the Tower. We will probably, in God's good pleasure, end up there anyway, but before that day comes when we can suffer for Christ's sake, we have lots to do. After all, it's not for nothing that I have disguised myself as a jewel merchant. We have jewels indeed to sell, and other jewels to gain, do we not?"

"Oh, that *was* a careless slip, *Mr.* Edmunds", said Ralph, looking at the same time disturbed and amused. "Well do I know the danger we run, and so, from now on, I'll never call you Father again; and perhaps you'd better speak roughly and sharply to me in the hearing of others so that they will think I really am just your servant. If you look on me in kindly fashion, as your affection may lead you to do, people will think that you are a very strange master indeed."

Mr. Edmunds sighed. "Yes, that's true. Well, so be it, Ralph. Here we stop being to one another priest and lay brother and dear companions in the Society that bears his holy Name, and become man and master. But we will still be brothers in arms, and praying for one another when we seem to be simply the one ordering and the other obeying. Here is my hand and my heart with it. God keep and guide us both, together or apart."

The two men took a long, brotherly look at one another, clasped hands, separated, and turned again to look at the dock, where a small crowd had assembled in the early dawn to see the latest ship in from the other side of the Channel.

Footsteps clattered on the deck behind them. Mr. Edmunds turned on Ralph with an impatient gesture. "And why do you stand here gawking like someone who has never laid eyes on the English coast before, man? Get you below and gather the luggage. You know that we will be hard pressed to get to London in time to meet the other merchants. I'll wait for you on the dock, and I'll have it out of your hide or your pay if you're late, do you hear?"

"Yes, master", mumbled Ralph, with a sidewise surly scowl. He was heard muttering to himself as he moved off.

"That's the way, sir", applauded the ship's captain. "You have to keep the servants in line these days. Put 'em in their proper place, I always say, or they'll run away with you. That's what the Queen, bless her, is doing these days with the papists—puttin' 'em in their place, though I, for one, think that their place is right smack in the Tower or on the gallows platform at Tyburn. A bunch of evildoers and traitors, that's what they are. And do you know what?"

"No, Captain," replied Mr. Edmunds, "you must tell me. You see, I've been long away, plying my trade as jewel merchant on the Continent. What have the papists been up to in England since the days of good King Henry?"

"Well," growled the captain, "most of the papists who wanted to become priests have had to go to seminaries—I think they call 'em—overseas. But some of them are still making their way back from the lands of the Frenchies and the Dutch, where they've been learnin' how to spread their superstition and their lies. They smuggle themselves over disguised—walkin' lies is what they are—like merchants and soldiers, and they are priests, who ought to be holy men and not base and false deceivers. Well, the priests that our good Queen allows still to work in the country are not like that."

"How do you mean, Captain," asked Mr. Edmunds, "the priests the Queen allows still to work in the country? Are there other priests who are not allowed to do their work of ministry?"

"Aye, that there are, sir", grunted the captain. "All the clergy were ordered to take what they call, if I remember the name rightly, the Oath of Submission, or something like that. Those who took it were allowed to continue holding their jobs, though, of course, they had to use the kind of service the Queen permitted. No more of those Masses and such; just a simple service all centered around the word of God."

"And what if some of the priests did not take the oath, Captain? What happened to them?"

"Well, they just had to retire. Many of them, I'm told, left the country. Many more took up living with some of the Catholic families. What they do with their time there, I have no idea. I reckon they spend most of it preaching to the papists about the Pope and such things.

"But the priests who took the oath aren't false betrayers and deceivers. They take their commands from the Queen, like any other good Englishman, and have nothin' to do with the Pope. So, like I say, keep your man under the bridle, keep the bit snubbed up short, and teach him to take his orders like anyone who knows his proper place."

He shot Mr. Edmunds a glance in which a little suspicion was beginning to dawn. The popish priests, he remembered he had just said, came over disguised "like merchants". Well, here was a merchant, but somehow he didn't have quite the look of a merchant about him. He looked—how *did* he look? He looked like a man who has other things to trade in than jewels. He looked—yes, that was it, he *did* look *priestly* for all his youth and good looks and obviously cheerful disposition. And hadn't this Mr. Edmunds been shaking hands with his "man" when the captain walked up behind them? Or perhaps the merchant had only been handing something to that Ralph.

The captain shrugged and stalked away. After all, this was not his problem, and if he started getting suspicious of all the Channel-crossers he carried, he would be a very busy man indeed. Besides, he grumbled to himself, what are the shore police for? It's *their* job to question the passengers, like that one a few weeks ago who was dressed like a soldier. A proper peacock he'd been, and I had my suspicions of him. But I wager he slipped through the hands of the police and is now in London, spreading lies and leading people into idolatry in the popish Mass.

Another shrug from the captain; he spat over the side of the ship and turned his attention and his uneasy suspicions into angry orders to the crew who were making fast to the dock. What troublesome times these are, he growled—and all because of an Italian Pope, and the King of France and the King of Spain, both of whom have their eyes on the fair land of England and would like nothing better than to head up armies to set the Pope on the throne. If only all the world were made up of brave and straightforward Englishmen!

Meanwhile, two Englishmen who would one day prove to the world how brave and straightforward they were, maneuvered down the gangplank to put their feet for the first time in many a year on the soil of their beloved England. Mr. Edmunds walked with as jaunty a step as one can on a slanting plank and looked around him with frank interest. Ralph, his man, carrying the luggage, looked up with surprise to hear him humming a tune.

"Rest here a bit, my man", said Mr. Edmunds

in a gracious tone. "I would stretch my legs on the beach after the trip in that foul and cramped ship. I'll take a turn to yonder rock on the beach and come back. By that time the searchers will be ready for us. If they come before I get back, tell them of me and my business here in the jewel trade."

Briskly he stepped off the dock and struck out for the large rock that jutted up from the water's edge. Ralph sat down on the baggage, folded his hands, and waited. His lips began to move. Was he irked with his master and muttering to himself what he thought of the merchant? The captain of the ship might have thought so had he been in a position to see Ralph. Another might have imagined that Ralph's lips were moving in prayer. At least his face did not bear the expression of one in a temper; it was the face of one at peace, of one who was perhaps thinking of other jewels than the ones that snuggled safely in Mr. Edmund's bags.

Mr. Edmunds' lips were moving, too. He had reached the large rock, which provided a good hiding place from eyes that might have been peering from the dock. He had fallen onto his knees, and his lips were moving in prayer. He, too, was praying about jewels.

"Lord Jesus," he said, "here begins the first battle of the war. Father Persons is ahead of me, feeling out the battle lines. How fitting it was that he came back home dressed like a soldier—and a strutting peacock he looked—for this will truly be a campaign. Give me and all of us in your army strength and joy and gaiety, so that we may win back to you all the Catholic souls who have been deceived by the teachings of the heretics, and that we may win many other souls, too, to know you and your Church.

"It cannot be long before we are hunted and tracked down, and when that day comes, I know there is nothing to expect save a mockery of a trial and death on the gallows. But before that day, help us to be strong and able, and to bring great peace of soul to all we meet. Help this poor-beset England, which I love.

"I renew the offering of my life which I made long ago to you when I pronounced my vows in the Society of Jesus. May I spend that life fully for your glory and for the conversion of England, which was once merry in you, but is now sad because it is on the road that leads away from you."

He rose, brushed the sand off his knees and trudged back, gay and humming once again, to join Ralph. Their eyes met, and each knew what was in the other's thoughts. All who may have seen them saw only master and man making their way to the headquarters of the police. The One to whom Mr. Edmunds had been speaking saw two "men"—his men.

So it was that Mr. Edmunds and Ralph landed on the Coast of England in June 1579. Who was Mr. Edmunds? Who was Ralph? Oh, the secret police in their headquarters at Westminster, the spies and informers who waited at all the ports and lurked throughout the land, snooping and ferreting to unearth the papists—they knew who Mr. Edmunds and Ralph were. They did not yet know them by these names, but they had descriptions of them.

They knew that Edmund Campion, a Jesuit priest, and Ralph Emerson, a Jesuit lay brother, were so tall, so stout or thin, had such-and-such a complexion, talked and walked in this or that way. They were watching and waiting. One day Father Campion and Brother Emerson would walk right into the trap, and what a blow that would be to the stubborn papists who still would not yield to the Queen's authority!

But this time, at least, Father Campion and Brother Emerson walked right through the trap, just when it seemed about to close on them.

When Mr. Edmunds and Ralph stood before the searchers at the port to declare themselves and what they had in their luggage, the authorities were on the lookout for a gentleman named Gabriel Allen. Gabriel was the brother of Dr. Allen, the president of the Catholic seminary at Douai, in what is now Belgium, from which many priests were returning to England in defiance of the ban and at the risk of their lives.

Gabriel, so the secret police had heard, was on his way home to visit relatives in Lancashire in the north of England, and the police were in wait for such a rich prize. Suppose he could be caught and "persuaded" to deny his Catholic Faith! What a way to discredit Dr. Allen and all his seminary priests!

It happened that Mr. Edmunds looked not unlike Gabriel Allen, and so, when he and his man Ralph stood before the police, what a smile of triumph lit up the face of the chief of the port's searchers. They had their man!

But alas for their hopes! Mr. Edmunds easily proved that he was not Allen. The mayor of Dover, before whom he and Ralph had been hailed, decided that he ought to send them up to London under guard anyway, just to be sure. Mr. Edmunds stood praying as men were sent to make the horses ready for the journey; he prayed to his patron, Saint John the Baptist, whose feast day it was. Suddenly, from the mayor's private office, an elderly man stepped out and said to the suspects rather roughly:

"You are dismissed."

Who was this man, and why had the decision been changed? Mr. Edmunds and Ralph never found out. But they wasted no time. Off they went to where they hired a boat to take them by the river route up to London. What a sigh of relief they heaved! The first stage of the dangerous journey was over. They had gotten behind the lines of the enemy. The great battle was ahead, and the great glory too.

The pleasant waters of the Thames and the green and fertile fields on either side, dotted with the white villages, did not look like a battleground. Only where the spires of the churches pointed their steady fingers to heaven was there a reminder that a great war was going on for the souls of the Englishmen.

And so, Edmund Campion, with his companion, came to London to take his place in the battle line. It was to be the place of a leader, of a giant, of a chivalrous hero, of a saint. Mr. Edmunds, the jewel merchant—Saint Edmund Campion of the Society of Jesus—was to become one of the brightest jewels in the crown of English Catholicism and in the roster of the Church's martyrs.

Father Campion and Ralph Emerson stepped down from the second boat they had been in since their sailing from Calais. The little Thames river boat had anchored at a pier in London. On the busy docks the crowds were milling and pushing; the cries of the boat ferrymen filled the murky London air; everywhere there was bustle and confusion.

As the two travelers stood looking around them for some guidance in all the hurly-burly, a young man strode up.

"Mr. Edmunds," he exclaimed, "give me your

hand. I have been waiting here for you to lead you to your friends."

The young man was Thomas Jay. He was a member of what came to be known as the Catholic Club. This was a good-sized group of young men, all of noble birth, all still staunch in their Catholic Faith, who had vowed that they would be at the service of the Catholic priests of the country. They served especially the missionary priests who were coming back to rally the Catholics to the defence of their Faith.

Father Campion grasped the hand of the brave young man and introduced him to Brother Ralph. At once the three were threading their way through the narrow and twisting streets of London. Thomas Jay cast many a backward and sidewise glance to see if they were being followed, but apparently the coast was clear. Whatever may have been the suspicions of the mayor of Dover, they apparently had not as yet reached the ears of the police in London.

Walking rapidly without giving the impression that they suspected they might be followed, the three were soon at the door of the house of George Gilbert in Chancery Lane. George was also one of the Catholic Club, though he had been raised as a strict Calvinist.

During his younger years, he had gone to Paris, where he had been converted to Catholicism by the Jesuit Father Thomas Darbishire. On his return to London, he put his great wealth at the services of the missionary priests. This was the young man, then aged twenty-eight, to whose care Father Campion and Brother Ralph were now turned over by Thomas Jay.

"Welcome back to England, Father Campion", exclaimed George Gilbert. "Father Robert Persons has told us to be ready for your arrival. He is away, visiting some of the Catholic families in and around London. But he bids you stay with us till he sends other word. Then he and you will sit down and make plans for the coming campaign. And, I assure you, you will have your work cut out for you, for Father Persons is on the go day and night. He's now in one disguise, now in another, so that even we, who have come to know him so well, hardly recognize him when he comes knocking at the door."

"Yes, I know;" said Father Campion, "he has always had the knack of acting, and now he has turned it to good stead in acting for the cause of our dear Lord. But say, George, is it not dangerous for me to bide in your house—I mean, is it not dangerous for you and the other members of the club? They were on the watch for me at Dover, and, though I was released then, I am sure that the police were not satisfied. The alarm probably has already gone out to trace the jewel merchant who went under the name of Edmunds."

George gave a hearty laugh. "Father, it's clear that you have indeed been out of the country for a long time. There is danger, yes; but things are so topsy-turvy that often there is less danger when one is, so to say, right in the lion's jaws. Do you know whose home this is? It belongs to Adam Squire. And who is he? No less than the chief of the police in London and son-in-law of the false bishop of London, whom the Queen has put up in place of the bishop authorized by the Pope. But we have bribed the pursuivants—as the police are called now after the French fashion—and we have little to fear so long as the gold finds its way into their hands."

"But, George," asked Father Campion, "doesn't that mean that the people, too, are confused? Are they all for the decrees of Elizabeth, by which they are not allowed to hear Mass and must reveal their knowledge of the whereabouts of priests? Or do they rebel against those decrees? What is it like in England now?"

"Father," answered George, "things are in a terrible state of confusion. Catholics are bewildered. Some will go to the services that Elizabeth has commanded must be the general rule. Others think they must in conscience stay away, though they have to pay enormous fines if they do not appear at their parish church every Sunday.

"Most of the older priests who were restored to their parishes under Queen Mary—bless her—

have not taken a firm stand against the new laws, and so, the body of Catholics do not know where to turn. Thanks be to God, we hope that men like you and Father Persons will draw up some plans of definite action for us. We are ready, all the Catholics I know, to do what we must for the cause of Christ and his Church, but we must have leadership."

Father Campion had listened with bowed head. He lifted it, gave a cheerful smile, and said; "That, George, with God's help, is what we are here for. We are to help turn the tide. It may seem a hopeless task, but we are sure, absolutely sure, of victory. It may not come today or tomorrow, but come it must and will. And so, we are happy, no? This is no time for heavy hearts, for we are on the winning side because it is God's side; and the heretics are on the losing side, because it is opposed to God.

"Well, more of this later when Father Persons returns and we get down to the plan of action. Now, do you have a bite to eat for Mr. Edmunds and his man? Come, Brother Ralph, let's break bread for the first time in England for many a year. We'll sup often from now on, I fancy, just leaning down in the saddle or catching a bite while the relay of horses is being brought up. Now let's sit and sup at our leisure, just as though all of England were welcoming us home."

"And the best part of England does welcome

you, Father", said George. "For the best part is still the part that holds with Christ and his Church. Eat well, Father Campion and Brother Ralph, for soon you will be out in the front lines, making the best part of England become the whole of England, restored to the unity of the Church and brotherhood of Christendom." And so Father Campion and Brother Ralph sat at supper with George Gilbert and others of the Catholic Club.

Calais and Dover were behind. The second rampart had been scaled. Here they were in London, and the whole of England stretched out before them, ready and ripe for their love and their labors.

Meanwhile, Father Persons was working his way from Catholic home to Catholic home to the north of London.

To the south, word was making its way up to the capital that a Mr. Edmunds had slipped through the hands of the police at Dover. Furthermore, the police had matched the description of Mr. Edmunds with that supplied by the spies who had seen Father Campion before he sailed. They knew that Edmunds and Campion were one person.

The alarm would soon be out and the jewel merchant himself would become a jewel. Anyone who found him would be richly rewarded.

It is small wonder, then, that a man called George Eliot sat in a small room in London and debated with himself. He had professed to be a Catholic and had been in the service of many prominent Catholic families. But he had got into trouble with the police, and though charged with many crimes, he had been convicted of none. However, he was in ill favor with the authorities and he was debating with himself how he could regain their good will.

"All that I know about the great families I have worked for", he thought, "doesn't seem to interest the police much. Perhaps they know as much as I do. But here, I believe, is my great chance. This man Father Campion—Mr. Edmunds, he calls himself—if I could only track him down and turn him in—*then* I might get back into favor."

He rose, gave the table a resounding blow with his hand, and growled: "I'll do it! I'll go to Lord Leicester and tell him I know how to capture Campion. Perhaps even the Queen will hear of my willingness to serve, and the reward will be bigger than merely getting back into the good graces of the authorities. I'll do it, come what may!"

He started, for it seemed that he heard echoing in the dingy little room a sad voice whispering, "Judas! Judas!"

About the same time Father Campion was saying to himself, yes, as soon as Father Persons returns we'll make plans for the great campaign.

Whether Eliot and Leicester or Campion and Persons would win, God alone then knew. Now, 400 years later, we know who won.

2

HOW IT ALL BEGAN

As Father Campion looked around at the young and eager faces of the members of the Catholic Club, all busy with their supper and with plans for the future, his mind went back some thirteen years and began to trace in memory the strange and gracious ways by which God had led him to this supreme adventure.

A bright summer's day in 1566 dawned on the university town of Oxford. Despite the fact that it was vacation time, most of the students and all the professors were still staying at the halls and colleges of the university. More than that, there was in the lovely old town a great stir of excitement. Crowds began to gather early in the morning and by noon time all the roads and paths in and about town were lined with an eager crowd.

"How soon do you think it will be?" could be heard on the lips of the people, who kept craning their necks to look off in the distance toward the main road that ran into town.

"Not too long now" would come the reply. "Her Majesty is a great one for being prompt, I've heard tell."

And sure enough, very soon could be heard the sound of horns and the clatter of hoofs, and the cries began to arise on all sides.

"Long live the Queen!"

"God save Her Majesty, Queen Elizabeth!"

Yes, at last the Queen was visiting the university. She had paid a similar visit to Cambridge two years before, and ever since, authorities at the University of Oxford had eagerly awaited her. They were now determined that they would give her a welcome that would make her soon forget what Cambridge had shown her.

One of the reasons the Queen made these visits to the great universities of the realm was to keep her eye open for likely young men she could summon to Court and put in positions from which they could advance and become her faithful officials. This was especially true in the church which Elizabeth had set up after she succeeded to the throne from which her father, Henry VIII, had kept up his fight with the Pope.

Many years before, Henry VIII had grown tired of his wife, Catherine of Aragon, and had been smitten with the pert beauty of a young woman at the Court, Anne Boleyn. The passion grew within his heart, and he cast about for a way to get rid of his first wife. He applied to the Pope for an annulment, claiming that his first marriage had been invalid. The Pope and many learned men all over England and Europe considered Henry's arguments, but finally the Pope declared that the first marriage had been in all regards valid, and that Henry was not free to marry Anne Boleyn.

Henry promptly flew into a rage. He declared that the Pope had exceeded his authority; that, from then on, he, Henry VIII, was the supreme head of the church in England in all things, temporal and spiritual as well. The Pope, he stormed, would have no authority in any way over English Catholics.

At once many of the courtiers and the King's Council agreed and added "Have you considered how wealthy the church is? Look at all the monasteries and cathedrals. They are filled with riches— gold chalices and monstrances, vestments that are worth a fortune, and all sorts of things that Your Majesty could convert into ready cash to make England still richer and more powerful. Why don't you take them since you are, indeed, the head of the church?"

And so started the grim years when the monasteries began to be closed. Monks and nuns, who had no way of making a living in the world, were thrown out of their beloved homes. Funds which the faithful for centuries had left in their wills to support the monasteries were taken over by the King. Soon England was overrun by hordes of dispossessed monks and nuns, all begging to keep body and soul together. But Henry would not stop; he had got the lust for money in his blood and it turned into a fever.

Many of the nobles, too, who had been commissioned by Henry to see to the execution of his orders, lined their pockets well. A whole class of society began to emerge which owed its wealth and prestige to the misery of the religious.

Henry did not at first bother much about church services. Most of the parish priests were allowed to go on celebrating Mass as they always had, administering the sacraments and preaching. But toward the end of Henry's reign, some of his ministers of state, who had listened to the Protestant doctrine that was coming more and more into England from the Continent, began to urge Henry to get rid of all remains of connection with Rome. They suggested that he change the services, suppress the

Mass, and deprive the people of the spiritual benefits of the Church of Rome.

Henry did not take many of these suggestions, but when his son, Edward VI, a young boy, came to the throne in 1547, the Regents, who governed for him, had their way. Priests all over England, unless they followed the new ceremonies that had been drawn up, were in danger of imprisonment. Edward died six years after he became King, and Mary, his half-sister, became Queen. She had never agreed with her father, Henry, in his fight with the Pope and his assumption of supreme power in the church in England, and she promptly restored worship to what it had been.

But Mary, too, was to die soon. In five years, she could not do much to restore the monasteries to their rightful owners, undo the great damage, or halt the movement that Henry had started rolling like a huge snowball to crush Catholic life in England.

Elizabeth was next in line. She was the daughter of Henry's second "wife", Anne Boleyn, and she inherited her father's determination to be supreme in the church in England. The laws opposing the Church and favoring Anglican forms of worship as they had been under Edward, were revived. A sad time began for the Church of Christ.

Up until 1570, the laws against the religion of the Church of Rome were not terribly strict. They were nothing like they were to become later, as we shall see in the life of Edmund Campion. Still, the saying or hearing of Mass, the saying of the Rosary and so on were forbidden under severe penalties, and all had to attend services which had been written to take the place of the Mass and other Catholic devotions.

As a result, many of the priests had retired. They lived in seclusion, often at the large country homes of Catholic landowners. Relatively few of the clergy went along with the "reformed" church which Elizabeth was bent on making the church of all England.

And so, on her journeys to the seats of learning, the Queen was always looking for young men who could be induced to be ordained in the new religion. Elizabeth was, to be sure, a patron of learning, but she had a keen eye for the practical, too, and it was most practical and pressing to find capable and compliant ministers of religion.

The cavalcade, then, wound into the university town. Every now and again, it would pause, and a professor from one of the colleges in the university would step forth and read an elaborate speech of welcome. On the day of her entry, the poor Queen heard speeches in Latin, in Greek, even in Hebrew, and, of course, in English. We can imagine that even the royal patience was somewhat frazzled and that the Queen was glad when the first day's welcome was over. Late in the evening she sank with a sigh into the regal bed prepared for her.

Her visit to Oxford lasted six days, but it was on the third day that the meeting occurred that was to shape the life and destiny of Edmund Campion. Years later it was to bring the Queen to a decision that must have cost her much and that gave another martyr to the glorious roster in the Church of Christ.

On Tuesday, September 3, the Queen sat listening to the various speeches and feats of learning that were being laid out before her like a too-rich banquet. It was all a little boring but part of the price for being a Queen.

All of a sudden, though, Elizabeth straightened in her chair. A handsome young man of twenty-six had bowed before her and asked her indulgence to begin his learned discussion to prove "that the tides are caused by the moon's motion". We can imagine that the Queen was not very much concerned with the moon and the tides, especially as she knew something about natural science herself. But we do not have to imagine that she looked at the young man with quickened interest; we know she did, because of what happened later.

The young man finished amid much applause, the Queen leading it. Elizabeth turned to one of her advisors. "Who is that young man?" she asked. "Find out all there is to know and report to me."

Who was he? He was Edmund Campion, born in London in 1540 and one of the most brilliant of the senior members of the university. He was most influential, especially among the younger men, who admired his scholarship, his literary ability, and above all, his gift for effective and moving oration. In fact, there was a whole group of younger scholars who went under the name of the "Campionists".

However popular and influential Campion may have been, he was a very confused young man at this period of his life. When he had taken his Bachelor of Arts degree at Oxford in 1560, he had been faced with a hard decision. He had to take the oath of supremacy or give up the life of study and teaching he loved. This oath was the one all in public life had to take. By it they acknowledged that the Queen was supreme over the church in England in both temporal and spiritual matters.

Now Edmund had not been raised as a Catholic. His parents apparently had yielded years before and were living in the rather slipshod way of many other Catholics. What is the use of getting excited? they asked themselves. This is all a temporary state of affairs, and one day the Queen will change her mind, or perhaps marry a Catholic prince, and then all will be as it used to be. Let's just wait out the present unpleasant state of affairs. This was how many Catholics felt and thought, but Edmund was not made of such lazy thinking and weak will.

Still, at the time, he adhered to the new church of Elizabeth. In fact, as it became clear that he was going to continue his life of study, he decided to be ordained a deacon in the new church. What agony of regret this cost him later, we shall see.

This was the young man on whom Elizabeth had set her eyes and her designs. When the background of his life and his present popularity and high success at Oxford were reported to her, she sent for Edmund and introduced him to Lord Leicester and Sir William Cecil, two of her most valued advisers.

"Master Campion," she smiled, "your performance here these days has been most pleasing and shows a ready wit and deep loyalty to our realm. These two good gentlemen have told me of your record and of your intention to go on to the ministry of our church. Pray remember these two good servants of the throne. If there is anything either of them can do to assist you, they will be happy— for my sake and for the sake of England—to be your patrons."

Edmund went down on one knee.

"Your Majesty is too kind, and these two noble lords are gentlemen one would be proud to have as patrons. I pray God for the good health of Your Majesty and the noble lords, and I will presume to call on their help if and when I may."

"You would do well to do so, Master Campion," the Queen replied graciously, "for they can do much to advance you. You may go now, but keep our wish in mind.''

Edmund Campion retired from the Queen's presence. But, as the months went on, he retired more and more into his own thoughts. The more he read in the early Fathers of the Church as he studied his theology, the more he began to see that the church Elizabeth had set up could not be the Church Christ had founded and of which the Pope of Rome had, since the days of Saint Peter, been the head. It was known among his friends that he was leaning toward the Catholic Church, and more than one of them urged him not to throw away all his hopes for favor in the Queen's eyes just for the sake of some "theological hairsplitting".

But Edmund was not a man to stop with half-truths. He had in him a streak of steel, a keen mind and a passion for the truth. After months of struggle and debate, he knew what he had to do. He was helped in making this sacrificial decision by the letters he got from Gregory Martin, a dear friend at Oxford, who had sailed across the Channel to the seminary at Douai in Flanders, and who was going to be ordained a Catholic priest. Gregory knew well Edmund's honest and generous soul, and he kept urging him to face himself and do what his study and his prayer would by now have shown him must be done.

Accordingly, in the summer of 1569, Edmund went over to Ireland. There he spent some time with the family of a young man he had taught at Oxford. In his spare moments Campion wrote *The History of Ireland*, which beautifully illustrates his literary skill—one of the talents that had put him high in the Queen's favor. The book is dedicated to Lord Leicester, whom Edmund still thought of as his patron. By now, though, the suspicion must have been growing in Campion's mind that if he went over to Rome, His Lordship might well, one day not far off, be his enemy.

In March of 1572 the rumor reached London that the King of Spain was planning an invasion of Ireland. This was set off by the crazy dreams of an adventurer, Thomas Stukeley, who had gone to Spain. Posing as a son of King Henry VIII, he had volunteered to lead the invasion force. There proved to be nothing to the scheme, but the rumors aroused dread and superstition. And Sir William Cecil, one of the Queen's advisers, who was in favor of being more severe on the Catholics, saw his opportunity.

He sent orders to Ireland that the laws against the Catholics were to be more strictly enforced, and that those suspected of leanings toward Rome should be hunted down and questioned. Edmund Campion had never been a man to hide his thoughts, and many of the English officials in Dublin had heard him express his doubts about the spiritual supremacy of Queen Elizabeth.

That very month Edmund started living the life of a fugitive. Little did he know that not many years later he would be one of the most sought-after fugitives in the long history of the persecution of Catholics in his beloved England. From March until May he slipped from the house of one friend to another, always being careful to leave no trace and to bring no suspicion on his protectors. In May he sailed back to England, where he remained concealed, waiting to get across the Channel to the Low Countries.

He appeared in public once, in disguise and under the name of Mr. Patrick. He was in the crowd at Westminster Hall to witness the trial of a Dr. Storey. This old gentleman had been picked up by the English secret police in Antwerp, where he had sought refuge in his declining years, and been brought back in chains to be tried for treason. Actually, his crime had been that he was a staunch Catholic under Queen Mary. He was executed most brutally on June 1, but by this time Edmund Campion was on board a little vessel on his way to Douai.

Edmund must have brooded, as he looked out at the choppy waves of the Channel, on the horrible fate of Dr. Storey. He had not waited to see it, but he could well imagine it, for he had heard accounts of other hangings, drawings, and quarterings. Above all, his thoughts ran on the charge of treason he had heard trumped up against the aged martyr.

"Treason!" he thought. "How can it possibly be treason to remain faithful to Christ and his Church—as all of Christendom has done these many centuries until the England I love rebelled against the Pope? If the Catholic Faith makes a man a traitor, then I shall soon be a traitor, for, if God help me, I shall soon be reconciled to Rome and repudiate the false ordination I so wrongfully allowed myself to receive. I shall make up to my Lord Christ for my weakness. So be it."

Make up? How fully and nobly and cheerfully! With what a spirit of chivalry, with what daring and superb leadership! "Campion the champion", some of the popular songs of the day would say of him later. Now Edmund was on the first steps of a long journey that would triumphantly show the world what champions are like.

Lord Leicester entered the Queen's presence. He knelt, rose at her command, and began in an angry voice:

"Does Your Majesty recall the young man Edmund Campion on whom you looked with such favor when you visited Oxford some years ago?"

"Indeed, yes", said the Queen, and her face

lighted up. "He was even here at Court for a time, was he not? I did not see much of him, but I well know what splendid talents he has. Is there some request you would make in his behalf? He chose you as his patron if I remember."

"Patron, patron?" stormed Leicester. "That I was, but see how he repays me. It is several years since he left Oxford and went to Ireland, and we have had our eye on him. Everyone knew that he was wrestling with himself, that he was attracted to the superstitions of Rome. But who would have thought that he would be so foolish as to throw away all Your Highness' favors and ruin his chances for advancement?"

"And has he indeed done that?"

"Yes, Your Highness, he has, and more. Why, even a year ago he dedicated to me a book he was writing on the history of Ireland. The dedication, I avow, was full of honeyed phrases. He refers to my noble qualities and all that sort of thing and professes that he will always be loyal to me. But now, what has he done and where has he gone? He slipped away from us in Ireland, and my watchers at the ports say they have news that he has gone over the Channel."

"Does that mean that he is going to become one of the seminary priests?" asked the Queen sharply.

"That, Your Majesty, we have not yet heard,

but it is sure that he will bow his knee to the Pope and be, as they say, reconciled to Rome."

The Queen leaned back, a look of disappointment on her face.

"And I had such great hopes for Mr. Campion", she murmured. "We cannot afford to lose men like him, my Lord Leicester."

"We have not lost him, Your Majesty. We will keep track of him every step he makes and everywhere he goes. If he ever returns to England, we will snap him up soon. Oh, no, we have not lost him."

"I did not mean in that sense, foolish Leicester. We may not have lost his body, but I fear we have lost his devotion and his will. I think we have not heard the last of Master Campion, and that when we next hear of him, we will be hard put to break his spirit. He is a champion, our Campion, and the stuff that heroes are made of."

Lord Leicester took his leave. The Queen remained plunged in thought. Did she picture in her mind already the day they might meet? Was she perhaps wondering who would be the winner in the tragic contest that was even now shaping up?

She shook the thought from her mind and turned to business of state. Edmund Campion, on the little Channel packet, dismissed from his mind the picture of the unfair trial of Dr. Storey, commended himself to God, and settled down to a nap in the brilliant sunshine and in the crisp sea breeze. If he dreamed, did he dream of what the future had in store for him? Whatever his dreams, they were dreams of peace, for he had found peace in his own soul. Before too long, he hoped, he might be bringing the peace of Christ to hundreds and thousands of other souls.

His brown hair was ruffled by the breeze. On his handsome young face, under the close-cropped beard, played the winning smile that would some day be famous throughout England almost as the trademark of the chivalry of Campion, the Champion.

3

TRAINING FOR THE GREAT DAY

E DMUND CAMPION trudged up the winding path
that led to the front door of the English College at Douai in Flanders. His heart was beating
fast in expectation. First of all, he said to himself,
here is where I shall be received back into the
Church; here is where I shall pledge the allegiance
I should never have hesitated to acknowledge.
Then, too, he recalled, here is where I shall see
some of my old friends again and meet the many
other young Englishmen who are training for the
priesthood so that they may return to England and
minister to those who so sorely need priests.

But Edmund hardly expected to see a dear friend

so soon. Who was this running down the path, obviously to meet him? As the hurrying figure drew nearer, Edmund's heart leaped with joy. Could it be—was it—Gregory Martin? Yes, it was!

"Edmund, welcome, welcome, my dear friend", shouted Gregory.

"Gregory, how in the world did you know I was coming right at this time? How good it is to see you after all these years!"

The two young men threw their arms around one another and laughed and tussled a bit in affectionate disguise of their real emotions.

"Why, Edmund," said Gregory, "the whole seminary has been waiting for you. It is not often that we welcome such a distinguished", and here he bowed low in impish reverence, "addition to our brotherhood."

"Gregory, you old hypocrite", protested Edmund. "You know as well as I do that when you arrived here, the whole seminary was agog to see the famous young scholar. You, I hear, have made a fine mark here at Douai, just as you did at Oxford when you and I were scholars and masters there."

"I hope so, Edmund", replied Gregory, and his young face grew sober and reverent. "For here, you see, the mark we make is of much more worth than the marks of scholarship we made at Oxford. Here we are preparing to be teachers of the doctrine of our dear Lord. At Oxford we were getting ready to teach only what Aristotle and Plato and other great human minds had thought."

"Well," he brightened up and clapped Edmund on the back, "I hadn't thought to greet you with a sermon. Come along now and meet your other friends. Richard Bristow is here, as you know. He never wearies telling us of how he was on the same side of the debate with you when the Queen made her visit to Oxford. To hear him tell it, you did all the debating and all he did was to sit there open-mouthed with admiration at your eloquence."

Chatting happily, the two young men approached the entry. It was the door to the seminary from which Edmund would leave in the not too distant future to take the road that would lead him to Rome and Tyburn. Gregory would not tread any such road, for he would remain at Douai, working with other scholars on the great English translation of the Scriptures which we know as the Douai Version.

Even before Edmund and Gregory stepped through the door and met the famous rector, Dr. William Allen, Edmund felt that he was in a place where most of the bravery and chivalry of England had been assembled. And how right he was he would come to know during the next two years.

This was the seminary which was the seed bed of martyrs. Young Englishmen could no longer study for the priesthood in their native land, and so those who could manage to flee from England came to Douai. A few years after the college was founded, it was sending back to England about twenty priests a year, and, by the end of Queen Elizabeth's reign, no fewer than 160 of them had met death for their religion.

Is there any wonder, then, that young Edmund felt that he was in the presence of the flower of England? From the day he began the life of a seminarian at Douai, the conviction grew in him that he, too, would one day pay the supreme sacrifice.

For two years, Edmund settled down to the quiet, yet intense, life of study, prayer, and teaching. He soon realized that he needed a longer period of training than he could get at Douai. So, with the approval of Dr. Allen, he left for Rome to apply for admission into the Society of Jesus, then only some thirty years old, but famous for its teachers and its missionaries. Members of the Society were already carrying the word of God to India, to China, Japan, Abyssinia, and Edmund prayed that he would be one of the first of the Society of Jesus to carry that word back to England.

In April Edmund was admitted to the Society, but England was still a long way off. He was sent first to a place called Brunn in Moravia and then to Prague in the September of 1574. After his novitiate and studies were completed, he was assigned to teaching. Edmund was an obedient Jesuit, and if he was told to teach, teach he did with all his heart. But how that heart was at the same time yearning for the life of a missionary in England!

Six years was a long wait, but the day came when Edmund, with eager hands, tore open a letter from Rome. It was written by Dr. Allen, in Rome on official business. In it was the great news that the Father General of the Society of Jesus had consented that some of the English Jesuits be sent back to England.

The Father General had only a handful of English subjects to choose from, and he knew well that in sending them back home, he was practically condemning them to death. But he had yielded to Dr. Allen's pleadings and now Father Campion was reading:

> Our harvest is already great in England. Ordinary laborers are not enough; more practiced men are wanted, but chiefly you and others of your order. The General has yielded to all our prayers; the Pope, the true father of our country, has consented; and God, in Whose hands are the issues, has at last granted that our own Campion, with his extraordinary gifts of wisdom and grace, should be restored to us.

Father Campion closed the letter, and his eyes shone with happiness. Not when he had proudly proclaimed his oration before the Queen at Oxford, not when she had offered him her favor and advancement in her service had he felt so joyful and exalted. He was being offered advancement in the service of another Monarch who was King of Kings.

It was in Rome that Father Campion learned that Father Persons was to go to England with him. They had been together at Oxford, but since Father Campion was six years older, they had had little in common, save the fact that Father Persons, too, had taken the oath of supremacy, had left England, and was also a convert.

Even though Father Campion was the older, he asked most earnestly that Father Persons be appointed his superior during their missionary work in England. He was too humble to want to have charge of anyone and, besides, he already saw in Father Persons the ability to plan and organize that was to make the work of the two Jesuits in England so astonishingly successful.

They had long conferences with the Father General of the Society and with officials of the Vatican. They were well briefed. Their work was to be one exclusively of "preserving and augmenting the Faith of the Catholics in England". They were not to enter into disputes with heretics, and, above all, they were not to talk about or treat with matters of state. They were not to allow any talk in their presence against Queen Elizabeth, and they were to recognize her authority in temporal matters.

Here, too, Father Campion met Brother Ralph Emerson, who was to be his companion in his first travels through England.

The day came when they were to begin the journey north to one of the Channel ports. What a day it was! With what excitement and happiness did the band assemble! There were about fourteen in all as they crowded into an assembly room where they were to have the joy of seeing the Pope and getting his blessing and instructions. The band knelt as Gregory XIII entered the chamber. The Pope looked lovingly at them all, but perhaps his gaze dwelt longest on Father Campion and Father Persons, for he knew all too well the great dangers they would soon meet.

The hand of the Pope was raised to bless them; the firm voice exhorted them to be faithful ministers of Christ and to bring his peace to the troubled realm of England; then the audience was over.

But other visits were in store for the missionaries. Before leaving Rome, they called on Father Philip Neri, already known as a saint. His blessing, too, descended upon them, and they were ready for the trip. A large crowd of well-wishers accompanied them to the edge of Rome, and leave-takings were shouted in great good spirit.

Lurking on the outskirts of the crowd were a few men who did not seem to join the excited and happy gathering. They did not seem to be in good spirits at all, and they were busy jotting down mental notes. They were the spies, the watchers, whom the head of the secret police in London had stationed at almost every port and in most of the big cities where English exiles lived. Week by week these reports made their way back to England. Hence, long before English Catholics, and especially priests, arrived from across the Channel, the Queen's officials knew they were on their way.

With the cheers and blessings of their friends in their ears, the missionaries trotted their horses away from the Eternal City. The first actual step toward the work they had long dreamed of had been taken.

They broke their journey at many towns along the way—towns where Catholics did not have to go about in fear of their lives. What a heartache it was to the priests to realize that in their own beloved England they would meet hostility and hatred, while now in the lovely towns of Italy they were being revered and saluted as heroes of Christ.

For eight days they stayed with the great and famous Cardinal Borromeo, bishop of Milan, who was one day to be canonized a saint.

It was hard to say who treated whom with most respect. The band of missionaries recognized in the saintly cardinal one of the great reformers of the age, one who was a leader in wiping out among clergy and laity alike the abuses that had done so much harm to the Church of Christ. The cardinal, perhaps granted by God some view of the future, saw in Father Campion—and indeed in all the members of the band—great and generous souls who were going into direct danger to win England back to that Church.

Finally the little band reached the Channel. There they separated, to make their way to the various ports, so that they would not arouse undue suspicions by embarking all together. Some went to Calais, some to Dieppe, some to other ports. Father Persons, Father Campion, and Brother Ralph waited at Calais, intending to cross over to Dover. Word came that the guard at Dover was so strict that they would surely be captured as soon as they set foot on land. But delay would have given the danger time to grow, so Father Persons decided to act at once. He dressed himself like a soldier, assumed a swaggering, boastful air, and sailed away. Father Campion and Brother Ralph were ordered to wait till Father Persons sent back word that it was safe to cross over.

Nine days passed. The long-awaited word came. Father Campion was to disguise himself as a jewel merchant; Brother Ralph was to pretend to be his servant. With many a good laugh at one another's expense, the two Jesuits assumed their roles. They strutted back and forth, addressing one another as "Mr. Edmunds", and "my man", so that they might get used to their strange titles and their strange garb. They knew only too well that they would have to be careful not to give one another away.

On June 20, 1579, Father Campion and Brother Ralph boarded the little vessel. But another wait had to be endured—a wait of four days in the harbor until the weather cleared. On the evening of June 24, the shouts of the sailors rang out, the lines were cast off, the packet nosed into the choppy waters of the Channel, and Father Campion was off to his brief and glorious ministry for the Englishmen he so loved. What were his thoughts? He has told us:

> As for me, all is over . . . I have made a free oblation of myself to His Divine Majesty, both for life and death, and I hope He will give me grace and force to perform it. This is all I desire.

4

THE SEARCH FOR THE JEWEL

T HE RINGING OF LAUGHTER and the thumping of tankards on the table brought Father Campion back from his reverie. One of the members of the Catholic Club had apparently just finished a merry tale or a good joke, and the peals of laughter would have made one think that here was a band of lively young blades concerned with nothing else than having a pleasant evening of it. With the threat of imprisonment and even death looming over them, they were still, as good Christian men, lighthearted and gay.

Lord Leicester sat at his desk and was not happy. Reports lay scattered before him, and every page of them shriveled up before his scowl. His Lordship was not pleased; in fact, he was in a rage.

"Here, man," he shouted at his secretary, "what is all this devil's work? The seminary priests were bad enough, but we took care of them, didn't we? That Maine fellow—what was his name?—oh, yes, Cuthbert Maine. Well, he said his last say at Tyburn back in 1571, when we had him hanged, drawn, and quartered. That might well have been the end of all this popery, but now there is another gang. What do they call them . . . the jesu, jesi—some name that sounds too much like the name of Christ to suit me . . ."

"Here it is, My Lord", said the secretary nervously, fingering through a sheaf of notes. "They are called the Society of Jesus (here he bobbed his head through long custom, though Lord Leicester frowned at this lingering trace of popery), and the popular name is Jesuits. It is a religious order, as Your Lordship knows, something like the Dominicans and the Franciscans and the other rabble that our Lord King, Henry VIII, cut down to their proper size and obedience to him—or, at least, he tried to . . ."

"Hold, man", cried Leicester, "King Henry did more than try; he succeeded. Where are the monasteries now in which the fat monks used to take their ease? The monasteries are turned to good use; the nobility of the realm now live in them and the lazy monks have long since been turned out to earn their bread in honest fashion. But what about these new religious men . . . the Jesuits, you called them?"

"Yes, Your Lordship. They were founded, it seems, just about fifty years ago by a Spanish grandee . . ."

"Faugh," spat His Lordship in an unlordly manner, "these Spanish religious fanatics."

"Yes, My Lord, but they do seem to have a way of starting things, don't they?" The clerk was seized with a fit of coughing—and just in time, too, for His Lordship was about to explode in anger.

"So, My Lord, the record shows that the founder of these Jesuits, one Ignatius of a place called Loyola—that's in Spain—died in 1556. But the curious thing is that within his lifetime his followers—fanatics, no doubt—were in the Indies. I read that one Francis Xavier got that far and died off the coast of China in 1552. Some are in Ethiopia; I find on the maps that that is somewhere in Africa. Some of them—how many, it is not stated—have penetrated as far as the realm of the great Mogul. That, the learned tell me, is in Asia."

"I congratulate you for the brilliance of your learning, sir," sneered Leicester, "but all I want to know is how, how in the name of all that's holy, did these . . . Jesuits get into England? Don't we have spies abroad to watch the ports from which

Englishmen, so-called, come back to England? Don't we—yes, don't answer that; I know we do—have watchers in the home ports to examine the merchants and the soldiers who come swaggering back, oh, so very English in appearance, but spies and traitors at heart?"

"Yes, My Lord, but . . ."

"But, but, but! But how did a soldier, who I now know is Father Persons—one of these cover-the-world Jesuits—and a jewel merchant, who is a Father Campion, get through?"

"Well, My Lord . . ."

"Well, well, well—but it is not at all well. I shall have to catch up now with these new ones, these Jesuits who sneak back into their native country, since we did not stop them at the ports. Who was that fellow you said wanted to see me?"

"A fellow called Eliot, My Lord."

"What's he done and what does he want?"

"He says he is a Catholic, My Lord, who, may I say, seems to think that perhaps he may serve Your Lordship and Her Majesty by perhaps, if I may say so, trading his Catholic Faith for something a little—so to speak—more valuable."

"Humph! Oh, well, show him in."

George Eliot stepped past the secretary, bowed to Lord Leicester, and started bartering away his soul and the life of Edmund Campion of the Society of Jesus.

Eliot and Leicester were making their compact against Christ and his Church. Would Campion and Persons make a compact strong enough to meet the challenge?

Father Campion was on his way to meet Father Robert Persons. The horses clattered their way up the road that led from London to Southwark, a suburb.

It was a clear and pleasant day, and the faces of the three men were clear and untroubled, though they were running the risk of capture and death.

"Father Campion," said George Gilbert, "do you know that you have already become something of a legend—a happy legend for the Catholics of the realm and a sort of legendary bugaboo for the enemies of the Faith?"

"Oh, come, George", replied Father Campion. "I am not quite that important."

"But you are. Lord Leicester and his men are trembling in their boots. And why? Because you Jesuits are something he does not know how to cope with yet. Your order is not yet fifty years old, and already it is known for fearlessness and vigor. Why, even now, if one says the word Jesuit, most of Leicester's people start looking for swarms of Jesuits all over the land."

"Well," laughed Father Campion, "I'm happy we strike such fear into the hearts of the enemies of the Church; but really, we are a small order and still have to prove ourselves, especially in this England of ours. You know, of course, that Father Persons and I are the first Jesuits to have been sent on the mission?"

"Yes, I do, Father, but I hope that you two are only the forerunners of the veritable army of missionaries His Lordship even now thinks he sees under every bed."

"I think we shall be, George", replied Father Campion thoughtfully. "And I fear—or should I say, I rejoice—that the army will suffer great casualties."

"That seems to be the glorious fate God has in store for them, Father", replied George, and then his face lit up. "But what a glorious band of martyrs they will be, and how proud of them will be the England of the future.

"But as far as the Catholics go, Father, you are truly a happy legend for them. Many of the families with great houses have their own priests living with them, of course, but how they will welcome the chance to be visited and encouraged by you and Father Persons! Please God, you two Jesuits will bring an end to the confusion under which many Catholics have been living. And I must admit that some of the priests have been as confused as the people they are trying to help. But you will show us what stand to take, and though it may be more dangerous and much harder, we will at least have easy consciences."

"Yes, that's what Father Persons and I hope to do. Our dear Lord once said that he came to bring not peace, but a sword. He does, of course, bring peace, but sometimes it is a peace that needs the sword first . . . the sword to cut away the past and to cut through doubts and confusion."

By this time, the little cavalcade—for Brother Ralph was in the company, though he had not uttered a word in all this conversation—had come to the door of a house in Southwark. Here Father Persons was hiding, eagerly waiting for Father Campion so that the great campaign could at last be planned in detail.

George Gilbert dismounted, signaled to Father Campion and Ralph to wait, and knocked on the door.

At various homes in London, George Eliot was knocking on doors, too. Where was a man called Mr. Edmunds, who was really the Jesuit Father Campion? Had anyone seen him? Did anybody know his friends? What about the members of the Catholic Club?

And why did George Eliot want to see Father Campion? Why, to hear the famous man preach, he said, for would not any good Catholic be thrilled to hear the man who had once had such a brilliant career at Oxford? And why was George Eliot interested in the Catholic Club? Well, would not any English Catholic with a drop of adventure and love for his Faith burn with eagerness to join that brave band?

Thus George Eliot began the career of deceit and pious pretensions that would one day succeed in shutting the trap on a man who did burn with the spirit of adventure in the service of his Lord.

5

CAMPION BRAGS

KNOCK, KNOCK, KNOCK thundered on the door.

The group of men fell silent. The babble of talk was cut off in an instant; every ear was alert; every head was turned to listen as one of the Catholic Club went to the door, gave the secret password, listened, and then turned back to nod assurance to the group. There was a sigh of relief; the buzz of conversation took up again, but not for long.

A whirlwind burst into the room. A big man, talking as he strode in, paused, glowered at the assembly, and boomed out: "Hah, and is this where the plotting papists are assembled?"

All stared at the Catholic Club member who had cleared passage for this man—a traitor, an informer? The young man shrugged, made a gesture that asked for silence, and motioned for Father Persons to speak up.

"Assembled, yes, as you can see. Papists, yes, and we are proud of it. But plotting—what plots can you suggest? If I knew, Mr. . . . Mr. . . . what is the name please?"

"Ho, ho, haw", chortled the somewhat wild-looking man. "I know the plots, and I say God bless every one of 'em. For they are plots to bring our dear Lord back into the realm of England, aren't they, and back hand in hand with the Pope—God bless him—just as Christ and Peter walked hand in hand? Oh, yes, I know your plots, and if Thomas Pounde has anything to say, they will win the day . . ."

Thomas Pounde! At once the group broke into welcoming laughter; they rose and crowded around the big man. Why, this was the Thomas Pounde who had been in prison—the infamous Marshalsea—for years. He had refused to knuckle down to the Queen's demands and attend the parish church in which he saw only a denial of all he knew the Catholic Church stood for. But how was he here? Had he been released from jail? Had he given in and denied his Faith, and was he now a spy?

Thomas caught the suspicion that began to peep from under the laughs of relief.

"No, men—and Fathers, whose blessing I crave—no, there's nothing suspicious about my being here. You see, I'm still in prison . . . ha, haw! We have ways and means of slipping a few pounds to the jailors—my name is Pounde, you remember—and so we are able to get out for a few hours. And why did I want to get out? It's really not too bad in Marshalsea; we can get food—extra food—brought in if we can pay handsomely enough for it; and all in all, it gives a man time to meditate a little and consider the state of his own soul."

"Welcome, Mr. Pounde", chimed in Father Persons. "We have heard what you have suffered for the Faith, and I'm sure that you will pardon us for the slight hesitancy."

"Ho, ho, Father, don't tell me. I know what the silence is like that descends when the knock comes at the door."

"It is rather frightening," put in Father Campion, "especially when one remembers what England was like back in the old free days."

"Ho," exclaimed Thomas Pounde, "from what I have heard you must be Father Campion. Your hand, Father, and your blessing. And this must be Father Persons; the other clergymen I know, and most of the Catholic Club know me, I think."

"Indeed we do, Thomas, though you have spent

so much time in prison that many know you only by name", said one of the members. "But what brings you here now?"

"Fathers," said Thomas, "I have heard that you two members of the Society of Jesus—may his name be blessed—"

"*In saecula saeculorum*", chorused the assembly.

"That you two Jesuit priests", went on Thomas Pounde, "are soon to start out to visit all or most of the Catholic homes in the north country. Do you know what's going to happen? The Queen and Lord Leicester are going to send out word ahead of time that you are here to act as traitors of your country and that you will be sly and wily enough to say that you have come back only to reconcile people to the spiritual authority of the Pope. They will say that in reality you are counseling people to revolt against the Queen and to be ready to receive the King of Spain when he comes sailing with a fleet to take over the realm. . . ."

"Oh, but Thomas," interjected Father Persons, "that is nonsense. We have strict orders not to meddle in politics . . ."

"Yes, Father," responded Thomas, "you may know that and I may believe it, but will the people, once the word gets around, skillfully planted by Leicester and his men, that you *are* traitors? If you are captured, you may be sure you will be put away where you will never be able to say a public word in your own defense."

"Well, Thomas," asked Father Persons, "what can we do about that? It's just a chance we will have to take."

"No, it isn't, Father, if you will pardon my saying so. I have had some experience with the secret police, and I know that the best move is to try to beat them at their own game. Here's what I suggest. Let both you and Father Campion sit down right now and write the reasons that have brought you back home, what you hope to be able to do, and what you are not going to do, namely, meddle in affairs of state. Let me have the documents and then, when the proper time comes—when you may be captured, I mean, though I hope to God that day never comes—I will see to it that your declarations reach the ears of every Catholic and every man of good will in the country."

"But that, Thomas," objected Father Persons, "won't convince Her Majesty or the Lords of her Council."

"No indeed it won't", growled Thomas. "They don't need any convincing . . . they *know* that you are here only for religious purposes, but you can be sure they will say in public anything else but that. At least, Fathers, the people of this realm—and especially our fellow Catholics—will be able to read the words you have written before capture, and the very honesty that will shine out in your statements will prove to them your loyalty. That is really what matters most, for the faith of some

Catholics might by then be wavering. If they believe that you were really spies, I fear that the dear cause for which you suffer will itself suffer great harm."

"There is sense to that proposal, Fathers", chimed in one of the members of the Catholic Club. "Lies will certainly be spread about you, but your word, written now when you are not under great pressure, will carry the very sound of conviction with them."

"And how shall we write it, Thomas?" asked Father Campion. "Do you suggest any form?"

Thomas Pounde looked at the two priests with love and sympathy. After all, he had had more experience than they with prisons and persecution. But he was not a priest and had never run the terrible risks he knew they would meet all too soon. How gallant and brave they looked—and were. His great, boisterous heart went out to them. He said in grave and measured tones:

"I would write your statements, Fathers, as though you were writing your last will and testament."

A reverent hush settled for a moment on the little group, and all fixed their gaze on the two leaders. Father Persons raised his eyebrows at Father Campion, and the latter nodded.

"A good scheme, I think. Fetch up pen and parchment, and we will set forth our reasons for coming back to home and danger."

There was a scurry of activity, and soon the silence of the little room was broken by the busy scratching of the two pens. In a half hour the two priests had finished their statements. Father Persons folded his up, carefully sealed it, and said to Thomas Pounde as he handed it over:

"I think it would be better not to reveal this till the proper time comes, Thomas—when the news is abroad that we have been taken. The whole plan might well lose its effect if it became known too early."

Father Campion said nothing, but simply folded his document and gave it to Thomas Pounde.

"Thank you both, Fathers", boomed Pounde. "These two papers will turn out to be immortal statements, I feel in my heart. And they will prove that you are loyal Englishmen and loyal Pope's men at one and the same time."

Thomas was an impulsive man, and when he clattered his way back into the prison at Marshalsea, he could not resist the temptation to peek into the document written by Father Campion. He did not dare break the seal on Father Persons' letter. What Thomas Pounde read made his heart leap with excitement. He pulled the document open and read through to the end.

He could hardly control his excitement, but he had to wait till the Catholic prisoners were assembled, as they were allowed to do at times in the prison. Then, with the air of one with great and important news, he rose and asked for silence.

"My dear friends," he said, "you know that I

got out for a while yesterday to go see Father Persons and Father Campion. I asked them, as we had discussed, to write down their statements about what they had come back to England to do, namely, to minister to the Catholics and bring back to the Church those who had fallen away. Well, I met them—where, I will not say—and made the request."

"And did they agree, Thomas?" a voice asked rather anxiously.

Thomas Pounde paused, cleared his throat, and responded with a seriousness that was unusual for him.

"They did, indeed. Father Persons sealed his note and I have not broken the seal, nor will I. But since Father Campion left his unsealed, I took the liberty to read it. It is a piece of writing that will make you feel like cheering. It is magnificent and brave and chivalrous and, oh, well, let me read you the ending. In the first sections, Father Campion states that he is a priest and a Jesuit, that he has come to preach the word, to administer the sacraments, to instruct the simple, to reform sinners, to confute errors. He goes on to say that he has been strictly forbidden by his superiors to deal in any respect with matters of state or policy of the realm.

"But, now, listen to this ending. The letter is addressed to the Lords of Her Majesty's Privy Council. Listen to Father Campion:

Many innocent hands are lifted up to heaven for you daily by those English students, whose posterity shall never die, which beyond seas, gathering virtue and sufficiency of knowledge for the purpose, are determined never to abandon you, but either to win you heaven, or to die upon your pikes. And as concerns our Society, be it known to you that we have made a league—all the Jesuits in the world, whose succession and multitude must triumph over all the practices of England—cheerfully to carry the cross you shall lay upon us, and never to despair of your recovery, while we have a man left to enjoy your Tyburn, or to be racked with your torments, or consumed with your prisons. The expense is reckoned, the enterprise is begun; it is of God, it cannot be withstood. So the faith was planted; so it must be restored.

If these my offers be refused, and my endeavors can find no success, and I, having run thousands of miles to do you good, shall be rewarded with rigor, I have no more to say but to recommend your case and mine to Almighty God, the Searcher of Hearts. May He send us His grace, and set us at accord before the day of payment, to the end that we may at least be friends in heaven, when all injuries shall be forgotten.

Thomas Pounde ceased. There was a dead silence, and then a long sigh from the assembled Catholics. Here was a voice of youth, a ringing call to hope and courage, a challenge, and a dare—just when it might seem that all Catholics in the country ought to be overwhelmed by discouragement and despair.

"It's not for nothing that Father Campion has been thought by many to have been one of the finest young writers when he was at Oxford", said one of the group.

"Aye, man", responded Thomas Pounde through the tears of pride and joy that dimmed his eyes. "And when you have a writer who is also a holy and brave priest, then you have a voice that will waken this poor country from her long sleep of heresy."

"What does Father Campion call his statement?" asked another. "Is there a title to it?"

"No," replied Pounde, "but I, for one, would like to call it *Campion's Brag*. That's a fine bold word; it brings up thoughts of a challenge and a dare and a bold, honest statement. And further, it will show Leicester and all his snoopers that we are taking new heart."

"A good idea, by our Lady", chimed in many. "*Campion's Brag*—a wonderful title." And so the wonderful document came to be known. But what happened when it came to be known? For it soon did. Copies were made and began to pass from hand to hand among the Catholics; many were smuggled out of jail. Wherever they made their way, they put new heart and new hope into the Catholics who were still faithful, and steeled many who had begun to waver.

And what happened when Lord Leicester and his men read it? They were more determined than ever to catch Father Campion, and Father Persons too—and the sooner the better. They knew that unless the Jesuits' work soon was brought to an end, their own job of making Catholics knuckle under would be harder than ever. And so the jewel they were after, Father Campion, was more precious than ever—all because impulsive and eager Thomas Pounde could not resist peeking into the note Father Campion had entrusted to his safekeeping.

6

THE JEWEL MERCHANT
WORKS NORTH

T HE TWO MEN stood at the door of the little
house in Southwark. The work of the meeting
was over and the various Catholics, priests and
laymen, had gone their separate ways. Their talk
with the two Jesuits, Father Campion and Father
Persons, had strengthened them in their fight for
the Faith. At the same time, the meeting had made
them realize more clearly their obligations.

Gone now were the old days of not knowing
for sure what they had to do. They knew now
that they would simply have to refuse to attend
any church services, since all services that were

allowed were heretical and forbidden by Rome. So, though their road was to be clearer, it was also to be harder. But all had said that they were ready and eager to show that their Faith was worth any sacrifice they would be called upon to make.

All this had taken place just after Thomas Pounde left with the precious letters from Father Campion and Father Persons.

Now these two men stood before the door waiting for their horses to be brought up. Father Persons had done missionary work north of London once before—just prior to Father Campion's arrival. But this was the first time Father Campion had embarked on the exciting and dangerous trip. What would he find? What success would he have?

"Well, Father Edmund," said Father Persons, "here we part for a while. We will meet again in London or nearabouts in a month or so. Meanwhile, give me your blessing, and, in token of our mutual remembrance, let us exchange hats."

This the missionaries did, and it was a custom they always maintained. Whenever they parted, they gave each other a blessing and swapped hats in order to be reminded of one another in all the trials and dangers they were sure to encounter.

They mounted and rode off. Father Persons was accompanied by George Gilbert, the member of the Catholic Club we have already met playing host to Father Campion in London. Father Campion had as his guide Gervase Pierrepoint, another young member of the club vowed to assist the missionaries.

Off they rode, each dressed like a fine gentleman mounted on a good horse and accompanied, apparently, by his manservant.

What were the two priests going to do? Where would they go, and how would they be received?

In London, George Eliot would have liked to be able to answer those questions. He knew by now that his quarry had slipped out of town, but Eliot was still busy—asking questions, getting descriptions, tracking down friends and acquaintances—slowly, slowly trying to draw in the net that one day would catch the jewel merchant Jesuit.

Father Campion worked through Berkshire, Oxfordshire, and Northamptonshire, always stopping at the house of some prominent Catholic, where he was welcomed in the following fashion. This account is taken from a letter written to Rome and telling how the Jesuits made their way through the countryside.

> When a priest comes to the houses of the Catholic gentry, they first salute him as a stranger unknown to them, and then they take him into an inner chamber where an oratory is set up, where all fall on their knees and ask his blessing. Then they ask how long he will remain with them, and pray him

to stop as long as he may. If he says he must go
on the morrow, as he usually does—for it is dangerous to remain longer—they all prepare for confession that evening; the next morning they hear Mass
and receive Holy Communion; then after preaching
and giving his blessing a second time, the priest
departs and is conducted on his journey by one
of the young gentlemen.

No one in these parts is to be found who com-
plains of the length of the services; if a Mass does
not last nearly an hour, many are discontented. If
six, eight or more Masses are said in the same
place, and on the same day (as often happens when
there is a meeting of priests), the same congregation
will assist. When they can get priests, they confess
every week. . . . A lady was lately told that she
should be let out of prison if she would just once
allow herself to be seen walking through an Anglican church. She refused. She had come into prison
with a sound conscience, and would depart with
it, or die. In Henry's days [King Henry VIII], the
whole kingdom, with all its bishops and learned
men, abjured its faith at one word of the tyrant.
But now, in his daughter's days [Queen Elizabeth],
boys and women boldly profess their Faith before
the judges and refuse to make the slightest conces-
sion even at the threat of death.

The adversaries are very mad that by no cruelty
can they move a single Catholic from his resolution,
no, not even a little girl. A young lady of sixteen
was questioned by the sham bishop of London

> about the Pope, and answered him with courage,
> and even made fun of him in public, and so was
> ordered to be carried to the public prison. . . .
> On the way she cried out that she was being carried
> to that place for her religion.

These were the brave people whom the missionaries
had come back home to help, and if they were
brave before, they were doubly brave after they
had seen the example of the daring priests. Both
Father Campion and Father Persons knew full well
the dangers they ran. Father Campion writes in
another letter to Rome:

> I cannot long escape the hands of the heretics; the
> enemies have so many eyes, so many tongues, so
> many scouts and crafts. I am in apparel [in disguise]
> to myself very ridiculous; I often change it, and
> my name also. I read letters sometimes myself that
> in the first front tell news that Campion is taken,
> which, noised in every place I come, so fill my
> ears with their sound, that fear itself has taken
> away all fear.

In almost every big home into which he was welcomed, Father Campion was always shown where
the "priest hole" was. This was a secret room,
cunningly hidden inside the wall, under stairs or
in any other place where it was unlikely that the
searchers would look. Here the priests would be
hurriedly hidden away when the rumor came that

the police were on the way to search the house. In such a little room, often only large enough to hold one priest stretched out on a cot, Father Campion would spend long hours, while overhead, in the corridor outside, or in the very room next door, he could hear the muffled tramp of boots and the tapping on the walls and floors.

As time went on, most of these hiding places became known, and there was nothing to do but take to the woods and forests when the police were on the trail. Many a night did Father Campion spend in the open, accompanied by some young gentleman of the Catholic Club who was guiding him. He would have no chance to say Mass, and his empty stomach would remind him that he was a hunted man.

Once Father Campion was in the courtyard of a large country estate, talking to a servant girl. All of a sudden came the sound of hoofs, and a band of searchers rounded the corner of the garden wall.

The young girl darted a startled glance at Father Campion. Quick as a flash, she gave him a great push that sent him stumbling and falling until he went splash right into a very dirty and scummy fishpond.

"Have you seen a gentleman by the name of Edmunds?" thundered out the leader of the band. "We hear he is spending some time here. If you are concealing him, you will be in great danger, for he is none other than the traitor Campion. Here, girl, do you know him?"

By this time Father Campion had climbed out of the pond, slimy and covered with algae and weeds. He looked like anything but a gentleman, let alone the "traitor" Campion. He sputtered and choked, while the servant girl shrugged her shoulders and said, "Well, there don't seem to be any gentleman around just now. Perhaps if you came back later. . . ."

The leader of the band, seeing no obvious quarry and anxious to get on with the hunt, barked a command to his men and off they whirled in a cloud of dust.

"Well, Elizabeth," said the dripping Father Campion, "that's certainly one quick way of putting on a disguise. Thanks for your quick thinking, and perhaps I'll be able to do as much for you sometime."

His quick, if weedy, smile and his boyish laugh told her, even more than if he had been openly serious, how close the escape had been.

Meanwhile, Father Persons had traveled through the northern counties of Gloucester, Hereford, Worcester, and Derbyshire, riding in disguise like Father Campion and meeting many of the same dangerous adventures. Everywhere he was welcomed with the same love and enthusiasm that Father Campion had experienced.

By October 1580, the two tired, but happy, missionaries were back in London, and it is easy to imagine with what joy they met and exchanged tales of what they had done and the great harvest they had reaped. Both of them could tell of the wonderful hospitality they had been shown at the great homes and could recount, with equal pride, how the humble people, too, had welcomed them with faith and affection. One of the happiest tales was Father Persons' when he told Father Campion what had happened in Stratford-on-Avon.

"One of the aldermen there, Father Edmund," he said, "is one John Shakespeare. He had for many years been slack in his religion and went to the new church. But I had a long talk with him and gave him that beautiful prayer we received from Cardinal Charles Borromeo. Do you remember how happy we were when the cardinal presented it to us?"

"Yes, truly, Father Robert. What a gracious man he is, and what a great cardinal! I fully believe that one day he will be proclaimed a saint."

"That lovely prayer, you will remember, was a last will and testament, and when I showed it to John Shakespeare, tears came to his eyes and he whispered to himself, 'And this is what I have turned my back on for so long.' With that, he asked to go to confession, made his peace with the Church and God, and begged me to leave the prayer with him. Just as I was leaving, I saw him conceal it over the rafters in his living room. I asked him why he hid it, and he smiled grimly. 'It would mean imprisonment to be found with it. It smells too much of the Church of Rome. But never fear, Father; now that I have found peace again, I won't slide back, and my family will be at one with me in being constant.' "

"What joy that must have been to you, Father Robert. That prayer is moving enough in its love and faith to bring many a man back to the Church and even make a saint of him. I can picture John Shakespeare, sturdy and a real English burgher, standing before you in his home and reading:

> I, John Shakespeare, an unworthy member of the holy Catholic religion, do . . . of my own free will and voluntary accord make and ordain this my last spiritual will, testament, confession, protestation, and confession of faith . . .

"Then John Shakespeare would have gone on in his reading to ask pardon for any murmuring against the Catholic Faith, and to pledge in most loving terms his fealty to the glorious and ever Virgin Mary, Mother of God; to ask that the signer be freed speedily from the pains of Purgatory and to beg the prayers of all relatives and friends.

"Truly, it is a most Catholic document, Father Robert, and I can well see why John Shakespeare felt he must hide it awhile."

"Let us hope", responded Father Persons, "that his children will know of it and live up to the Catholic sentiments that are so strong in it."

And so it came about that John Shakespeare, the father of William, the immortal playwright, was reconciled to the Church. This was but one of the great consolations the missionaries had, though, of course, they did not know that William would one day be a glory of the literature of England and of the world.

They did not know, either, that George Eliot, the spy, would also one day be famous—or infamous— as a betrayer of his Faith and the missionaries. They did not know George Eliot at all. But he knew them.

He knew that they had been in the north of England; he had a list of some of the houses they had visited, and his men were making the rounds, questioning, questioning, getting details of what the priests looked like, learning that they were back in London.

Eliot and his men came hurrying back to London, hoping this time to close the net and capture not only the jewel merchant, but the slippery Father Persons as well. Campion, however, was still their big prize, their jewel, for by this time his name was on everyone's lips. The Catholics and those who longed to come back to the Church spoke of him to bless and praise. Those who hated the Church mentioned him only to curse him, for he had aroused in the people such a wave of enthusiasm and he was so daring and resourceful, that it looked as though all the work of King Henry VIII and Queen Elizabeth might well be undone.

But how to catch Campion and put him out of the way? That was the question that made Lord Leicester feel furious and frustrated every time he dwelt on it—and he dwelt on it many a time in the coming months.

7

THE PRESSES ROLL

Lord Leicester was furious for an added reason. There lay on his desk a little booklet called *Ten Reasons*. It was written by Edmund Campion and, worst of all, it was *printed*. It had come off a printing press; it had not been copied by hand.

Where could the Jesuits—those two phantoms named Campion and Persons—have possibly set up a press? They could not by any chance have used one of the presses of known publishers, for the government had complete control of them. They must, therefore, have a press of their own. Where was it? How could it be discovered?

The long arm of the police went into action again,

and eventually the printing press was discovered and destroyed, but not before Father Campion had issued a bold challenge that was to stir up the whole of England. It was also the act that most intensified the chase and led to his arrest.

Father Campion's famous *Brag* had made its way about the country by word of mouth, or by hand-written copies. Soon after its appearance, a number of pamphlets, written to refute it, had appeared from the pens of heretical clergymen. Father Persons, who was the planner where Father Campion was the doer, was convinced that the Catholics had to have some way to answer quickly the accusations against them. If an accusation was repeated long enough, and often enough, without reply, then people began to believe that it was true.

So Father Persons had gone scurrying about in London, trying to buy a printing press, paper, ink, and all the other things needed. He had great trouble, for he could not buy all the equipment in one place—and would not if he could, for that would leave too many clues by which he could be traced.

At last Father Persons managed to get together everything he needed to set up a press. He was ready to start publishing the work of Father Campion that would be even more effective than the famous *Brag* in refuting the heretical teachings of the Anglican church and in strengthening the spirit of resistance among Catholics.

But a further problem arose. Where in the world would the press be housed? The police were constantly searching the homes of known Catholics, and a press was not a thing that could be tucked away in some little closet. Where would Father Persons find a large enough, and a safe enough, place?

He took his problem to the young men of the Catholic Club, and one of them suggested a Mr. Watfarer, who lived some five miles away from London. Father Persons rode out one fine spring day to have a little talk with Mr. Watfarer.

He found the house in a somewhat secluded spot. He dismounted, knocked on the door, and said a silent little prayer while he waited. He was going to ask Mr. Watfarer to do a brave and dangerous thing, and he prayed that God would inspire Mr. Watfarer to be generous.

The door opened, and Father Persons began:

"Mr. Watfarer, I have been told by some young gentlemen—you know the ones I mean—that you have a large room I might be able to rent. Could I come in and discuss the matter with you?"

Mr. Watfarer sized up Father Persons slowly and cautiously. Strangers were not to be accepted too readily in England these days, as one never knew when the secret police would come knocking at the doors of Catholic families.

"Step in, sir," said Mr. Watfarer finally, "and

we can talk over the matter. Perhaps you would sip a glass of wine as we discuss terms."

"Right heartily, sir", responded Father Persons. "One does get a little dusty and dry on the trip from London."

When Mr. Watfarer had poured out two glasses of wine, Father Persons stretched out his right hand and, while looking Mr. Watfarer straight in the eyes, made the sign of the cross over the glass and said in a clear voice the Latin grace before meals: "*Benedic, Domine, nos et haec tua dona. . . .*" "Bless us, O Lord, and these thy gifts which we are about to receive, through Christ our Lord, Amen."

Mr. Watfarer's gaze held steadily against Father Persons'.

"I take it, sir," he said, "that you chose this means to tell me that you are a Catholic. You are doubly welcome. How can I be of service to you?"

Father Persons gave a little sigh of relief.

"Yes, Mr. Watfarer, I am a Catholic. More than that, I am a priest, a Jesuit priest. My name is Father Robert Persons; perhaps you have heard of me from members of the Catholic Club. They are the young gentlemen I referred to, and it is they who commended you to me."

"Father Persons?" gasped Mr. Watfarer. "The famous Father Persons? What a delight to meet you, Father, and what an honor, too. Ever since the day you and Father Campion came back to England, every Catholic in the country has been dying, I imagine, to have the chance to meet you."

"Thank you, Mr. Watfarer", laughed Father Persons. "It does begin to look as if we are turning into some kind of legend. But I have a very grave request to make of you. Would you be willing to do something for Father Campion and me—and for the cause of the Catholic Faith in England?"

He raised his hand before Mr. Watfarer could speak the eager answer that obviously hovered on his lips.

"Before you answer, let me say that what I shall ask you to do will plunge you into considerable danger."

"So much the better, Father", cried Mr. Watfarer. "I have led a rather untroubled life here, away from London. When I hear what things many of my fellow Catholics have had to suffer for the practice of their Faith, I begin to feel as though I have been lazy and not generous enough with God. What would you have me do?"

"One of the greatest and most effective steps we can take", responded Father Persons, "to further the cause of the Faith is to print refutations of the errors that are spread abroad in the form of books and pamphlets. Father Campion's *Brag*, as it is being called, has done great good, but he is now engaged in writing a longer work, which he calls *Ten Rea-*

sons. In it he sets forth ten arguments to prove that the Church of which the Pope is the visible head is the Church our Lord founded. It would be slow and almost impossible work to have his book copied by hand in sufficient numbers to be distributed all over the land. And so, I have managed to get together all I need to set up a printing press."

"A press?" echoed Mr. Watfarer. "That's a bold venture indeed, Father." He broke into a chuckle. "You two Jesuits are certainly stealing the heretics' thunder, aren't you? Imagine how they will fume to see *printed* answers to their false teaching."

"Well, Mr. Watfarer, here is where you can do a great service. The room I spoke to you about . . . would you be willing to provide it to us as a printing office? I would like to set up the press here, in your house, if you will run the great risk. Will you allow me, for the sake of the Faith?"

Mr. Watfarer did not pause long. He thrust out his hand, grasped Father Persons' hand, and said sturdily:

"I shall be proud to have the press here, Father, and to join you in the risk. You have talked about the danger *I* may run, but you have not said a word about the constant danger *you* are in. I think it a blessing that I may be able to share the danger with you."

He went down on his knees. "Give me your blessing, please, Father. It will be the first I have had in a long time, and it will help me to serve in your work faithfully and bravely, if the danger threatens."

Father Persons smiled in admiration and thanks. He raised his hand, and into the soul of loyal Mr. Watfarer descended the blessing of Almighty God, Father, Son, and Holy Spirit.

For the next week or so the police would have noticed, if they had been on the alert about the doings at the home of Mr. Watfarer, that many large and bulky packages were being delivered at his door. Little by little, Father Persons began assembling his press in the room Mr. Watfarer had provided. Soon all was ready, and all that had to be done was to wait till Father Campion sent the text of his *Ten Reasons*.

Even so, the days were not all serene as Father Persons waited with his press in readiness. Every now and again the alarm would go out that the police were in the neighborhood, and the priest and members of the Catholic Club would have to slip away and hide.

This left Mr. Watfarer alone, with the press standing in the basement as evidence that he was engaging in business that the government would certainly ask questions about. But God was good to the bold venture and, despite the frights and hidings, the press was not discovered.

Meanwhile, Father Persons had sent Father Campion north again, into Lancashire and Yorkshire. The services of a priest were needed there and had long been clamored for.

Once again Father Campion made his rounds, baptizing, saying Mass, preaching, everywhere bringing joy and new strength to Catholics. In addition, he was able to get a little time to finish his work on the *Ten Reasons*. Late at night, after all the rest of the household was in bed, Father Campion would be bent over his paper, busily scratching away. Finally the work was done, and Father Campion sent the manuscript down to London to Father Persons.

Into the press room Father Persons burst with a jaunty step. Several of the members of the Catholic Club were there, as they had been for several days, waiting to get to work on printing the *Ten Reasons*.

"Here it is, gentlemen", sang out Father Persons, waving the sheaf of papers. "Set the presses in motion, set up the type, lay out the sheets, prepare the ink! We are about to give the heretics the surprise and the shock of their lives. These *Ten Reasons* will be, I warrant you, ten thorns in their sides. If the Church owes Father Campion gratitude for writing this refutation, she owes you gallant gentlemen deep thanks, too, for running the great risk of getting the *Ten Reasons* printed. God will bless you, and future Englishmen will thank you for it all."

Now it happened that Father Campion was at the home of William Harrington at Mount Saint John in Yorkshire when word came that he was to leave, finish his journey through Lancashire, and return to London to give the book *Ten Reasons* a thorough proofreading before it was printed.

It was a dreary day in March when young William Harrington, son of the master of the house, knocked on Father Campion's door and handed him a sealed letter. After Father Campion's smiling "Thank you, William", the young man still lingered, shifting from one foot to another and obviously wanting to ask some questions. Father Campion had been with them twelve days, and William had been quite taken with him. He knew something about the Catholic Club, and his young and chivalrous heart was leaping to join that noble band and serve the missionaries.

Father Campion looked up from the letter he had broken open and was reading.

"Yes, William, what is it you are aching to ask me?"

"Oh, was it that evident?" young William replied with a grin of embarrassment. "I guess it must have been. You see, Father, what I would like more than anything in the world right now . . ."

"I wager I know what it is, William."

"You do? How could you?"

"Oh, young William, I have noted how your

eyes light up whenever our conversation turns toward the young men of the Catholic Club."

"I don't know about my eyes, Father. But ever since Mr. Tempest brought you here twelve days ago, I have thought of him. I saw how brave he was while leading you through dangers and spies, just so you could work as a priest among us. I have not been able to think of anything save what I would give to be able to be so brave too, for you Fathers and for our Lord. Could I possibly be one of the club? I think I could be brave too."

"That I know you could, William. But look you, son, we priests determined when we first started this dangerous work in dear England that we would take as members of the club only men somewhat older. The young are apt to be too brave, if you catch my meaning; they are apt to take foolish risks. But the way to beat the enemy and give them the slip often means taking the fewest risks necessary."

"But I would be prudent, Father; I would, I know."

"Yes, William, perhaps you would. But, you know, there are dozens of young men like yourself who would like to join the club, too, and perhaps they would not be as careful as you. Yet, if we take you into the club, we will open the door to those other dozens, don't you see?"

Poor William! What great things he wanted to do for the Fathers and Christ! He gulped down his disappointment, nodded glumly and was about to go when Father Campion stopped him. He flung his arm about the young man's shoulders, gave his merry laugh, and said:

"But William, don't lose heart. You know, I think that one day you will do even greater things for Christ than just guide some poor hunted missionaries about England. It seems to me," and here Father Campion grew very quiet and serious, "it seems to me that you may be called one day even to do the greatest thing for Christ. . . ."

William gazed at Father Campion with a wide and incredulous stare.

"Do you mean, Father, that perhaps I may even be called on to give Christ everything—everything . . . ?"

"You would be ready, would you not?" asked Father Campion very quietly, with a look of deep and brotherly love in his frank eyes.

"Yes, Father", whispered William, with brave young lips that trembled just a little. "I think I would because I have met you."

In May, Father Campion was back in London. What another happy reunion with Father Persons and the young men who had helped get *Ten Reasons* ready for the press! What tales of successes and what happy laughter over narrow escapes! What a sense of triumph, for though the lives of Catholics were getting harder and harder, and the fines for not attending the Anglican church higher and higher, there was, all over the country, a sense of unity. There was, due mainly to the toil of the two missionaries, a sense of being on the winning side—God's side—such as had not existed in the country since the days of Henry VIII.

But the laughter and the telling of tales did not last long, for there was work, great work, to be done. Father Campion checked every word of his book, and especially the references to Scripture, for the heretical clergymen put great store by knowledge of the Bible. If they caught Father Campion in one little slip, one little inaccuracy, how they would hoot that here was no scholar, as he indeed pretended, but an ignorant priest who was deceiving the people.

As Father Persons directed, Father Campion made sure all was correct. Then the little hand press groaned and creaked, and day by day the mound of printed pages grew. They were stitched into little booklets, and one day all the workers straightened their weary backs, wiped their brows and smiled at one another. All was ready. Now to get the booklets out and into many hands; then to sit back and see how furious the enemies would be. Not only had the Jesuits given them the slip again, but they were reaching the minds and the hearts of the people as never before.

Oh, it could not be long, thought and prayed Father Campion, before every former Catholic in England would be strong enough to practice his religion openly. It could not be long before every sincere non-Catholic would see the truth of the *Ten Reasons* and admit that there was no church that did not have and acknowledge the Pope as head. Either that, he knew, or it would not be long before he reached the end of his brief stay in England.

After this booklet had made its appearance, spies would be doubled and tripled, he knew, and the next time he went on a journey to preach and say Mass and administer the sacraments would most likely be the last time. After that, there would be only one other journey he could possibly take. He shuddered to think of it, but while he felt the fear, he blessed himself, turned his thoughts to his Lord Christ in the agony of the garden and murmured, "Not my will but thine be done."

It was an early Monday morning in 1581—June 26, to be exact. The next day would be commencement day at Oxford University. All the dons— the professors—all the students, brilliant and proud in their robes, all the friends and relatives, proud of the proud students, would be there for the great day.

As usual, the ceremonies would start with services in the church of Saint Mary. There would be a sermon by a famous preacher, and then all would go to the Senate House, where the degrees would be conferred. Yes, it would be a lively day, and many a speech, many a sermon, would be devoted to telling the people how the traitorous missionary priests from overseas had been foiled, and how England was at peace and happy under the new religion that Queen Elizabeth had set up.

"But they are all in for a great surprise", thought Father Hartley, as he jogged along the road to Oxford on his horse. He laughed to himself and patted the bundle that bumped on the saddle behind him. "Just wait till they see what is in here, and will their eyes pop!"

He laughed again, hustled his horse along a little, and began to hum under his breath.

"Dash it all!" He broke off his humming to mutter, "I must be getting infected with the same spirit that dwells inside the handsome face and figure of Father Campion. Here I am, riding right into the jaws of danger, and I find myself singing. Well, it's not a bad thing. Lord knows we were sad and glum long enough under the persecutions. No matter what Her Majesty the Queen and Leicester and others call the bad days, they *have* been persecutions. They still are—and even worse. But somehow, since Father Campion and Father Persons have been with us, things don't seem as bad.

"So, on to Oxford, Nellie, my good mare, and let us give them all the surprise of their lives when they assemble tomorrow morning for the commencement."

Father Hartley hummed again. The horse took up the pace, and soon in the night skies before them loomed the spires and towers of the university town.

Leaving the well-ridden roads for fear of meeting guards, Father Hartley skirted the town till he came to a little-used path. There he tethered Nellie, took the bundle from her back, and walked stealthily through side paths and narrow streets till he came to the dark bulk of Saint Mary's church. He knew where there was a little side door always left open. He found it; he tried it; good! It was unlocked.

He crept into the church. It was pitch dark. No longer did the little light dip and rise before the Blessed Sacrament; there was no Blessed Sacrament on the bare altar without a tabernacle. There were no votive candles before the images of our Blessed Lady and the saints; there were no images in the gaping niches.

But there were still pews. Father Hartley waited till his eyes became accustomed to the dark. Then, feeling his way so as not to make any noise—there might be some sexton or warden drowsing in the sacristy—he put his bundle down and opened it. Father Hartley took out what it contained and began to put into each pew things that looked like little books. He covered the whole church. At least one little booklet was left in every pew. He picked up his sack, genuflected out of force of habit before the main altar, crept out the little door, stole back to Nellie, mounted, and rode away.

"A good night's work", he hummed to himself. "I would love to see some faces in the morning. Thanks to you, Father Campion, for having written the little surprise I have just planted; and thanks to you, Father Persons, for having gotten it printed. You two will have all England talking and agog tomorrow as they have never been, not even when they read Father Campion's marvelous *Brag*."

This was how Lord Leicester came to be staring in rage at the little booklet before him on his desk. He bellowed for his secretary. The poor man came slinking in, for he knew from the tone of his Lordship's voice that he was in for a hard time.

"How did this thing get here? What have the police been doing that such an insult to Her Majesty could actually be printed? What do you know about it all, and if you say you don't know anything, I'll have your head . . . what . . . ?"

"Pardon me, Your Lordship, but the police have done something about it all. Several of the men who were connected with the printing press are already taken, and they are in the Tower, where, I imagine, ways can be found to make them talk."

"So—and that's all that has been accomplished? We have caught some of the helpers *after* the work has been done? That's not enough. We have to stop the job *from being* done. This booklet will give great heart to the papists; they will think that *we* are on the defensive."

"But, Your Lordship, the man Persons is a sly one. He it was who set up the press and got the pamphlet out. And every time we try to track him down . . ."

"Not Persons, man, but Campion. Persons may be the planner and therefore the more valuable man, but Campion is the man who stirs the public imagination. *He* is the man we have to capture. We can take care of Persons later. Where is that man— what was his name—Eliot, who was detailed to track down Campion? Get him and bring him in."

"Yes, Your Lordship."

So George Eliot had another conference with Lord Leicester. He showed His Lordship the list of names of the families with whom Campion had dwelt during his latest tour of the north counties. From that list they were able to get a good idea of where Campion might be staying the next time word came to them that the Jesuit was on his rounds to the north.

The net was being drawn tighter. It would not be long now before its strings would be drawn closed. Then the jewel merchant would know that the precious wares he had been selling to the Catholics of England were not rich enough to save him from the rack and the gallows.

8

THE LAST TRIP

ON A DAY IN JULY 1581, Father Campion was on his way out of London. His route took him by the gallows at Tyburn, the place in the city where criminals were executed and where, since the persecutions of the Catholics, many a brave soul had laid down his life for the Faith.

As he passed the grim structure that looked so much like a cross, he paused, removed his hat, and prayed for a moment because, as he thought, it *did* look like a cross, and because many martyrs had suffered there. Did he also have a feeling that he would soon be seeing again the cross of Tyburn?

He put on his hat and continued north. He was

on his way to collect some papers he had left at the house of a Mr. Houghton in Lancashire. Then he would go farther north into Norfolk on another round of apostolic visits. As Father Campion jogged along, with Brother Ralph again as his servant, he stopped short and said to Ralph:

"We are not far along the way. It has just struck me that we will be passing by the home of the Yates in Berkshire. Let's return, therefore, to ask Father Persons' permission to stay awhile with the Yates. They have long been after me to visit them. Mr. Yate is now in prison in London for his Faith, but his old mother lives at Lyford Grange with two priests who are in hiding and some nuns who were thrown out of their convents by the police. It would be a great act of charity to stop there."

"The two priests, Father Ford and Father Collington, take care of all the spiritual needs of the household, but I fancy they would welcome the company of a new face, and the good Yates and all the household have been eager to see the new missionaries. You might think, Brother Ralph," he laughed, "that we were some sort of wonder-workers. Anyway, we will perhaps put new heart into them all, for the very fact that we have returned to England from overseas may come to them like a breath of sea air."

"Very well, Father," answered Ralph, "but I doubt that Father Persons will give you the permission. The Yates' home is well known by the police, and they will certainly be on watch for you."

So Father Campion and Brother Ralph returned and put the matter before Father Persons. Father Persons pursed his lips and thought for a while.

"Very good, Father Edmund," he replied, "but I know how generous and thoughtless of self you are. I don't want you to stay any longer at the Grange than is absolutely necessary. Here is what I will grant. Brother Ralph here will be your superior; you will consult him if ever the doubt arises that you ought not to tarry longer. Brother Ralph, will you be prudent and restrain Father Campion's zeal?"

"I'll try, Father," responded Brother Ralph, "though I don't think it's fitting for a lay brother to give orders to a priest."

"Tut, man," laughed Father Campion, "I could not be subject to a better superior than to my little Ralph."

"So be it, then", concluded Father Persons. "Tarry a while at the Grange, but be ready to move north when Brother Ralph thinks a longer stay would be too dangerous."

The people at the Grange had been agog for several days. The famous Father Campion was coming; he would spend some time with them; they would all be able to hear his famous sermons. Was he

not, after all, the priest who had written the *Brag*
and the *Ten Reasons*? What a stimulus it would be
to their faith to see and hear him in person!

Father Campion gave them all they had wanted,
but he stayed only overnight. The next morning
he left, conscious of the danger he would run if
he stayed longer in a home that was well known
by the police for being ardently Catholic. He seemed
well on his way into Norfolk and was sitting at
an inn near Oxford with his "man", Brother Ralph,
when Father Ford, who had obviously ridden hard
from the Grange, burst in.

"Father Campion," he cried, "you really must
come back to the Grange. Despite all our best efforts
at secrecy, word got around in the neighborhood
that you had been with us. Catholics from all over
the area have assembled, clamoring to see and hear
you. They would be crushed if they knew that
you were so near and yet would not come back
to them."

"Well," said Father Campion, "I am not my
own man. Little Ralph here, my dear Brother
Ralph, has charge of me. You will have to apply
to him."

Brother Ralph flushed, shifted in his seat, tried
to look elsewhere, but could not avoid the burden
of responsibility that had been put on him.

"Well", he hesitated, but protests from Father
Ford drowned out his voice.

"Look, Brother Ralph," he exclaimed, "you can ride on and get the papers Father Campion needs. Meanwhile, he will come back to the Grange over the weekend, meet the dozens who want to see him, and be ready to leave when you return. Don't you see that is what Father Persons would have wanted too?"

Brother Ralph glanced at Father Campion, who barely nodded his head in agreement. After all, what was the risk? Just a few more days in which to do God's work, and then they would be on their way into the far north.

"All right, then", said Brother Ralph, turning to Father Campion with an assumption of great authority. "You may stay just until I return."

"Thank you, little Ralph," replied Father Campion, "and you will never regret the permission you have today given me."

Regret it? Brother Ralph would remember to his dying day that he had been one of God's instruments in making Father Campion a martyr and a saint.

Father Campion and Father Ford clattered up the drive leading into the Grange. Father Ford was glowing in triumph at having been able to get Father Campion to come back. He little thought that he was leading Father Campion back into the very trap which would finally snap shut to hold him fast.

As they dismounted and entered the house, where the large crowd of those who had missed Father Campion the day before were gathered, the priest was amazed and delighted to see among them his young friend, William Harrington. Mrs. Yate had a son, John, and he and William were good friends. Just the day before, William had ridden up from Mount Saint John to Lyford to spend the weekend with John and to tell him of the wonderful Father Campion, who had inspired him so much.

William ran forward with a glad shout: "Here is Father Campion now, everyone", as though all did not know who the cheerful young priest was.

"Well, William, it's good to see you so soon again. I did not know that you knew the Yates."

"Yes, Father, I have been good friends of theirs for a long while, especially of John, who is about my age. I have come to spend the weekend with John, and though I know you will be too busy to have much time for us, perhaps you will be able to tell us something of life in the seminaries on the Continent. We both feel drawn to the priesthood and, perhaps, if you think we might aspire to it, to become Jesuits and return home to work for the conversion of England."

"God bless you for the generous thought, William", said Father Campion. "And I will try to get a little time with you, but now I must put myself at the service of these good people who have assembled to hear me."

Father Campion was conducted to the chapel in the house, where he immediately preached a sermon to the audience of some twenty or thirty who had been thirsting so long to hear again the word of God—especially from one of the famous and brave missionaries. The two young men, William and John, sat entranced and felt their hearts thrill within them as they heard the tones of confidence and gaiety with which Father Campion told them that the cause of Christ would surely win in the end.

For two days Father Campion was busy hearing confessions, talking privately to those who wanted to ask his guidance, preaching, and in general putting new heart into all. He did find time, too, to tell William and John what life was like in the service of God as a priest.

Meanwhile, the pursuit was drawing closer and closer. In the peace and joy at the Grange, nobody suspected that the jewel merchant was soon to be captured and start his last journey to London and Tyburn.

The traitor, George Eliot, felt that his work was almost at an end. Still on the trail of Father Campion, Eliot had made his way into the same county. On July 2, he was staying at a place called Haddon. On that day and on July 4, he pretended to be a devout Catholic and heard Mass. As soon as he could, he had the two priests who had celebrated the Masses arrested and sent down to London to be tried. And it was in this fashion that he was determined to trap Father Campion. He would hide behind the mask of piety; he would pretend that he wanted so very much to attend Mass once again. Then, when he had proof that Father Campion had been the priest who celebrated the Mass— snap—the trap would close!

On Sunday, the 16th, some sixty people, including students from Oxford, were assembled to attend Mass and hear the famous Father Campion preach. It was early in the morning, and while the little congregation knelt peacefully and happily at silent prayer, while Father Campion vested and made ready to start the Holy Sacrifice, there was a knocking at the main door. The cook of the Grange got up from his knees and went quietly out to see who the latecomer was.

It was George Eliot. The cook some years ago had been a good friend of his, but he did not know that Eliot was now a spy. He exclaimed:

"Why, George Eliot! How long a time since I have seen you! What brings you here? Whatever it is, it is good to see you again."

"And I say the same, Master Cook. But let us save talking about old times for a little later. What I am really looking for is a chance to hear the blessed Mass again. You know how difficult and dangerous it is these days. But this is Sunday, and surely in a large mansion like the Grange here, there must be some priest who manages to slip in and celebrate the Holy Sacrifice and then be on his way again before the police get wind of his visit."

The cook smiled knowingly, but glanced suspiciously at the man who accompanied Eliot.

"Well . . ." he hesitated. "Well . . . perhaps I ought to talk with you privately."

"By all means. Wait here, my man, for just a moment."

Eliot and the cook went into the hall and closed the outer door.

"You'll soon see why I was so careful, George", whispered the cook. "Do you know who the priest is who is just getting ready to start Mass?" He paused dramatically. "It is none other than the famous Father Campion; you know, the man who wrote the *Brag* that has made the heretics so hopping mad."

"Father Campion!" exclaimed Eliot in an awed tone. "But what good luck for me! What a joy and an honor to receive Communion from the hands of such a man. Please, Henry, go beg of Mistress Yate permission for me to come in and join the worshippers."

"That I will, George, though I may have some trouble in persuading her. She has to be very, very cautious; there are many spies around the county these days."

"There are, of a certainty, Henry; but you know me. While you beg permission for me, I will just go to the door and dismiss my man. I will be back in a moment and then—oh, I do hope that I will be allowed to see and hear Father Campion."

The cook ran off on his charitable errand. Father Campion finished vesting and began the Mass. Eliot came back; the cook met him and said that permission had been granted. The traitor entered the chapel, knelt down, and followed the Mass with all appearances of devotion. He even seemed to be very moved by the sermon Father Campion preached. It was the ninth Sunday after Pentecost and Father Campion's text was "When Jesus drew near to Jerusalem, he wept over it."

All this time, the man Eliot had sent away was riding at a gallop to the nearest sheriff, for Eliot had whispered to him:

"Ride fast to the nearest police headquarters and tell them I have papers authorizing me to command in the Queen's name that the sheriff collect an armed force and come at once, for we have in our grasp a priest—and not any ordinary priest, but the traitor Campion."

Eliot's man rode hard, with visions of reward in his eyes. Eliot kept up the acting all through Mass, but when it was over, and all assembled for the meal that followed, he refused somewhat rudely to attend and strode out of the house. Many an eye followed him with suspicion and uneasiness.

Who, after all, was this stranger and how had he gotten in? Where was he off to now?

The tension relaxed when Father Campion, having finished his thanksgiving after Mass, came into the dining room and sat happily with his friends and brethren in Christ to break bread after the Bread they had just received. Young William Harrington and John Yate sat together at the foot of the table and hung on every word that fell from Father Campion's lips. The happy gathering had no suspicion of the danger that was fast closing in on them.

George Eliot had bolted from the house, mounted his horse, and was thundering down the road his man had taken just a short time before. At a turn some distance from the Grange, he met the sheriff with the armed force. He pulled up in a cloud of dust and shouted:

"We must make haste, men. The traitor, Campion, is now at meat, but he is to be on his way as soon as he is finished. We will surround the house and watch every exit while the sheriff here and I demand entrance and start the search. Men, this will be a great day! We have caught Campion, the brag maker! He'll brag no longer, I warrant you. Follow me!"

"Jesus wept over Jerusalem." How he must have wept over the soul of another Judas, George Eliot. But how he rejoiced that his jewel merchant was not far off now from winning the greatest jewel of all—martyrdom for his Name.

9

THE NET CLOSES

WILLIAM HARRINGTON AND JOHN YATE were
standing at an upper window of the Grange,
looking out over the meadows on this hot July
day. They had been talking of how movingly Father
Campion had preached that morning and how they
would love to be able to do as much for the Church
when they grew older.

"But how sad it is", said William, "that Father
Campion will not have long to do more."

"What do you mean, William? He is still a young
man and in the best of health. He will work for
years throughout the length and breadth of England
and leave a multitude of converts behind him."

"No, I'm afraid he will not—and so is he, though I do not mean he is actually afraid. He knows, John—and I certainly feel—that it will not be long before the net closes around him. And then? And then—what fate will be in store for him? A false trial and cruel death at Tyburn. Believe me, he knows that. I have seen it beneath the gaiety in his eyes and underneath his happy laugh."

"But why do you think that that fate will befall him so soon, William? He may be able to give the searchers the slip for years."

"I don't think so. For one thing, I believe that stranger who was with us at Mass this morning was up to no good. Did you notice how quickly he slipped away before the meal?"

He broke off with a start and gave an exclamation. "Look down the road there. See? See the cloud of dust? And it's moving this way. I warrant that when we can see through it, we will find the stranger there with a band of police. I feel it. I think we had better sound the alarm. We will have to spirit Father Campion out of the house with all haste."

"There won't be time, William", exclaimed John. "We will have to hide him in the priest hole. Come, there's no time to waste."

The two young men hurried off to raise the alarm. They burst into the room where Father Campion was talking to Lady Yate and others, some of whom were just preparing to take leave.

"The police are at the door!" cried John. "The stranger must have been a spy. And they are so close that they will soon have the house surrounded. Father Campion, we must hide you; there is no time to escape into the woods."

"Be quiet, son", commanded Mistress Yate gently. "We will let Father Campion make his own decision. It is his life that is at stake. Father, what is your wish?"

Father Campion had remained calm amid all the confusion that had broken forth at the alarming news. He said immediately:

"If it were at all possible, I would slip out of a side door and be off. If I am caught here, it will go hard for all of you and especially for my dear hostess and her family. Let me take a look."

He strode to a window from which he could see the road leading up to the house and the paths that ran through the garden. As he looked, a group of men turned a corner and began to scatter. Some obviously were on their way to cover all the entrances to the house. Two of them strode quickly to the main entrance.

Father Campion had no more turned back from his inspection than there came some thundering blows on the front door, and those within could hear the muffled shout, "Open, in the name of the Queen! We have search warrants and know that the traitor Campion is within. Open, or we break down the door!"

"Come, Father", said Mistress Yate, still calm and unruffled. "Let me show you to the priest hole. And you, Fathers Ford and Collington, you must hide with Father Campion, for though he is the great prize the Queen wants, her police would dearly love to lay their hands on you as well."

With great calm and dignity Mrs. Yate led the three priests to the secret hiding place. It was a small chamber built very cunningly in the wall over the gateway. It contained nothing except a small bed. The three priests entered; the secret door slid into place. There was no light for fear that a glimmer of it might betray the priest hole; they could hear nothing, after the sound of the retreating footsteps died away, save their own breathing.

"Fathers," whispered Father Campion, "let us now hear one another's confession, for it may well be the last we shall ever make."

Turning so that he might whisper in the ear of Father Ford, Father Campion made his confession and received absolution. We may well wonder what penance he was told to perform. Could it have been just to offer up to God the present danger and inconvenience? The other priests confessed to him and then there was nothing else to do but settle down and wait. They prayed silently and no doubt dozed a bit, but there could be no talking.

All through the long summer afternoon, in the stuffy heat of the hiding place, they lay and heard the sound of boots, the knocking of pikes and swords on walls, the muffled commands of Eliot and the sheriff.

At last all sounds of the search ceased. Finally there was a knocking on the secret door—a peculiar knock which was the password to let the priests know that the searchers had gone. Slowly the door moved back, and there stood the two young men, William Harrington and John Yate, with grins of triumph on their faces.

"You have done it again, Fathers", exclaimed William, though he had eyes only for Father Campion. "You have given them the slip once more, and it looks as though you will be able to continue bringing Christ back to his people."

"Well, William," said Father Campion, "if we have, it's because of the quick thinking and fine acting of all here, not least yourself."

William beamed at the praise before he remembered to look properly modest.

By this time Mrs. Yate and the rest of the household had crowded around the priests, laughing and chatting in their relief. The danger was over.

But was it? Outside the house the band of searchers had not yet mounted their horses. They were arguing with Eliot, or rather, he was raging at them.

"By the Lord Harry," he was seething, "we will go back into that cursed house and really give it a searching. Do you call what we have done all this livelong afternoon a search? I don't, and I know what real searching is. I have done enough of it to give everyone of you lessons."

The members of the search party were, after all, neighbors of the Yates and had had no love for the job. They had been forced to obey Eliot because he did have the Queen's warrant. They looked at him with no particular love, and the sheriff growled:

"We have caused good Mistress Yate enough trouble, and on a wild goose chase at that. We have done all we are going to do. Come, men, let's get home and leave good Master Eliot here to the rest of his dreams of favor in the Queen's eyes."

"Stop!" shouted Eliot. "The warrant I have says not only that we search, but that we shall break down walls and partitions. I will read you that portion of the document."

He pulled a parchment from his pocket, opened it with a flourish and began to read. But he hesitated a little, and one of the party slipped behind his back and glanced over his shoulder. Eliot was "reading" from a blank page.

"Look you, sheriff," shouted out the spier, "there is no warrant here to break down the walls; Eliot is making it up."

There was a growl of anger from the party, but Eliot was equal to quelling it.

"In the Queen's name," he barked at the poor

sheriff, "I command you to arrest that man and send him bound to London as an abettor of the Jesuits. He will get what he deserves at the hands of the warders at the Tower."

This did the trick. Frightened that the same fate might befall them if they refused to follow all Eliot's orders, the band agreed to go back and search as he would command them.

The priests, their hosts, and friends had been so busy rejoicing over their "escape" that they had not noticed the return of the searchers until there was again a thundering on the door and the harsh command to open.

There was not time to get the priests back into the hiding place they had just left, and so they were spirited to another which opened from a room toward the top of the house. Brave Mrs. Yate, after telling the searchers, and particularly her neighbors, what she thought of them for returning to make a wreck of her house, demanded that at least she, because of her age, be given a good night's sleep. It was allowed and, with great canniness, she had her bed made up in the very room which opened into the second priest hole.

Sometime during the night several of the household tiptoed into the room. Father Campion slipped out of hiding and, with his usual thoughtfulness for others, said a few words to comfort them. As he was going back into his little cell, somebody stumbled. One of the search party who was on watch in the lower part of the house came charging up the stairs, followed by the awakened Eliot. The priests were still here; now they would be caught!

When the searchers burst into Mrs. Yate's room, only the old lady was gently snoring in her temporary bed. All others had slipped away and the three priests were back in their narrow room of security.

And it was a room of security all the next morning and until late in the afternoon. By that time, even Eliot was willing to concede furiously that Campion and the other priests had given him the slip.

Eliot was descending the stairs, ready to give up, when he noticed a chink of light showing in a wall of the stairway.

"I've been right", he shouted in a loud voice, and, seizing a crowbar, he ripped into the wall. He pried and pried and stones and boards fell. On a bed lay the three priests: Campion, the great prize, and Fathers Ford and Collington, not so great a catch, but minor jewels in the crown of Eliot's treachery.

"I have found the traitors", shrieked Eliot. There was hubbub all over the house. The Catholics came running with cries of sorrow and alarm; the searchers tumbled up the stairs to aid in the capture.

The three priests rose and calmly and "courteously" (says the record of their capture) yielded themselves.

Young William Harrington and John Yate, seeing that they could do no good, and both now looking forward to the day when they might continue Father Campion's work, had slipped out a side door and were well on their way to William's home at Mount Saint John. William would see Father Campion once again; John never saw him again, but both had so well caught his cheerful and undaunted spirit that they would come one day to share the great prize that was so nearly in his grasp.

Meanwhile, Father Campion addressed his captors:

"Gentlemen, we shall go with you peaceably, for indeed we have done no wrong. If our trial be a fair one, we shall quickly prove that, but if it be a prejudiced farce, and we be tried only for the fact that we are priests and have preached the gospel of our Lord Jesus Christ to Catholics and those who ought still to be Christians, then we shall probably never meet again until we all gather happily together in heaven. At any rate, these good people have done no harm. Take us three priests, but let the rest of the household go free."

He might as well have spoken to one of the battered stone walls. Along with the three priests seven gentlemen and two servants were taken and made ready for the trip to London. We shall lose sight of these other prisoners later on in this story, for our tale is about Father Campion, but many of them were as brave as he and went to the same terrible, but glorious, ending.

For three days the captives were kept at Lyford while word was awaited from the Privy Council at London what should be done with the "traitors". Finally word came that they were to be sent under heavy guard to London to stand their trial. They made three stops in the journey to the capital. At one of these, Eliot, much puffed up by his victory, though most of the other guards despised him, feeling Father Campion's eyes resting thoughtfully on him, said:

"Mr. Campion, you look cheerfully on everybody but me. I know you are angry with me for my work."

In a low voice, but with deep compassion in his tone, Father Campion replied:

"God forgive you, Eliot, for so judging of me; I forgive you and in token thereof, I drink to you, and if you will repent and come to confession, I will absolve you; but large penance you must have."

Eliot turned away, a sneer on his lips. "I don't believe he forgives me", he thought. "I know I would not forgive one who had done me a like turn." Deep down in his heart he knew that he was speaking falsely. He knew that Father Campion had forgiven him, and it took the edge off his triumph, but only an edge. After all, the reward he was going to get, he dreamed, would be more than enough to restore him to a complete sense of triumph.

At the second stop, Father Campion noticed in the crowd that had assembled to see the famous Jesuit a man he recognized as a servant of Father Persons. His superior and dear friend, Father Persons, was staying at a little town nearby and had wished to come and see his companion, but friends would not allow him to. Instead, he had sent a servant. When Father Campion noticed the man, he gave him a wink and a smile but was careful not to let any of the guard, and especially Eliot, see that he had recognized this link with Father Persons.

The servant lingered until the band of captives and their guard were out of sight. Then he sadly took his way back and reported to Father Persons.

"Father Campion is still the carefree gentleman, Father Persons. He did not seem at all cast down and was chatting with his fellow captives and joking with them. You would have thought that he was on his way to London to meet dear friends for a celebration."

"And indeed he is, Peter," replied Father Persons, "the dearest friends of all. He will meet our Lord, and all the saints and angels, and, in particular, all the holy martyrs. Before many a week has passed, we shall be able to pray through the intercession of Father Edmund Campion, priest and martyr. Remember this and tell your children, so they may tell their children, that England is not lost to the Faith while men like Father Campion come back and cheerfully give their lives that Christ may return again to this once merry land."

There was, for all Father Persons' cheerful response, a note of sadness in his voice. He felt then that he would never be called upon to share the glory and the passion of his dear friend. And his premonition came true, for shortly after this he was recalled to Rome and was employed by the Society of Jesus and the Church in diplomatic missions to the end of his days.

Finally, the prisoners and their guard reached a place called Colebrook, some ten miles north of London. There they were ordered, by a letter from the Council, to remain the rest of Friday, July 21, so that they could get an early start on Saturday and enter London just when the crowds, out for their Saturday shopping and marketing, would be able to see the disgrace of the "traitors".

Their guards were commanded to treat them differently, too. No longer would the prisoners ride free and at their ease. They would be used to show the Londoners just what happened to those who defied the commands of the Queen in matters of religious conformity.

When they started their journey through the

city—they were paraded from end to end of it—
the crowds laughed, and many hissed and booed
the prisoners. They rode with their elbows tied
behind them, their hands lashed together in front,
and their feet secured underneath their horses' bel-
lies. Father Campion was singled out for further
ridicule by having a paper pinned to his hat, which
read: "Campion the Seditious Jesuit".

As the parade passed a section of London called
Cheapside, they trooped before a cross standing
in the marketplace. It had been battered and defaced
in the religious troubles, but it was still a cross.
Father Campion raised his eyes to it, bowed his
head as far as he could, and tried to make the sign
of the cross on himself with his fettered hands.

Some of the crowd pressing close to see the famous captive hooted and jeered.

"The papist sign won't save you from the cross
that waits for you on Tyburn, you traitor."

"Tie his hands tighter."

"He'll bow to the stone of the cross, but he won't
bend his stiff neck to the Queen."

"Haw, haw, but soon he won't have a head on
top of his neck to bow with at all."

Such were some of the hoots and catcalls, but
some of the people looked with respect and sympathy, not to mention shame. Was this England, that
an accused man could be treated as though he had
already been tried and found guilty? Did he have

the ghost of a chance to get a fair trial? What would happen to the country if things like this went on? Could England ever again be thought of as part of Christendom if priests and good Catholics were persecuted and put to death just because they were priests and good Catholics?

These thoughts were in many minds, but they remained locked up there because it would have been dangerous to express them. But Father Campion would express them very soon and in a way that gave, even when he was in his last hours, new heart and courage to those he had come to serve.

Yes, England could still be thought of as part of Christendom, so long as other Campions would follow to carry on his work. And they did follow. From Campion's day to this, priests have continued to preach Christ and his Church, and lay people have continued to follow. Persecutions and martyrdoms would continue for more than a hundred years, but peace would finally come to the Church in England, and with peace, growth and vigor.

Did Edmund Campion know this, or even think of it, as he heard the iron doors of the prison in the Tower of London close behind him? He knew with all his faith and all his generosity that the Church would not and could not fail. In his humility, though, he never began to realize how much he would be responsible for the heroism that would mark the English priests, secular and religious, who would follow him.

Just before the prison gates closed behind him on July 22, 1581, Father Campion turned to the guards who had brought him to the gates.

"Thank you, gentlemen," he said, smiling, "for all your courtesy. You have treated me in kindly fashion, as far as was in your power. If perhaps you have done anything harsh to me, may God forgive you, as I forgive you. But truly I must say that I am more concerned for the blindness of your hearts than I am irked by anything that has befallen me. Look to your souls and pray that God will give you light to see where his truth lies— whether in the false teachings of the heretical church or in the blessed doctrine of Christ and his Church, which has but one leader and head on this earth, the Vicar of Christ, the Holy Pontiff in Rome . . . I shall pray for you all and for the Queen and all her ministers, for, whatever befall me, I am a loyal Englishman. If I die at Tyburn, it can only be because I am a priest and a Catholic."

The guards shifted their feet uneasily. Some looked ashamed and worried; others glared in hatred. Father Campion turned and walked into the gloomy interior of the dread prison. Clang! went the doors behind him. His long agony had begun.

"There's one thing I know for sure", said one of the guards as they tramped away from the Tower.

"There is a brave and gracious gentleman. They say he is a traitor, but I don't see how a man like that can be. It's a puzzling business, I say, and I don't know what to make of it."

But Father Campion knew what to make of it. He was on his knees in the dark and damp cell, asking God for strength to continue the good fight to the end. What that end would be he saw as clearly as a sunburst before his eyes. He shivered in dread and horror; from lips that were generally so laughing and happy, but now were stretched over his clenched teeth, came the words: "Not my will but thine be done."

10

IN THE TOWER

VISITORS TO THE FAMOUS TOWER of London look about them with a lively curiosity. It's a quaint old building and the famous Beefeaters, the official guides in their flamboyant uniforms from the Middle Ages, add to the charm of the picturesque scene. But even the visitor of today, as he is led down into the gloomy cells and along the stony corridors, begins to feel a little shiver of dread tingling along his spine.

What must the prisoners of the sixteenth century have thought when the doors of the Tower closed upon them? Few men—or women—ever came out of the Tower in those days to tell what it was like inside. Most who emerged came out to go to their death at Tyburn. When Father Campion knelt in his cell, praying for strength to be brave and loyal to Christ to the end, he knew enough about the treatment that was most likely in store for him to have every reason in the world to be filled with fear.

He had heard of the Pit, in which a prisoner might be confined for weeks and months. It was a cave running down for twenty feet and in absolute darkness. He knew of Little Ease, a cell so constructed that a prisoner could not stand upright nor lie down at full length.

Another form of torture was the Scavenger's Daughter. This was a broad hoop of iron which ran between the legs and over the head and forced the prisoner to remain in a crouched-over, cramped position. When this was maintained for days or more, it frequently was impossible for the poor prisoner ever to stand upright again. Before Father Campion's vision rose, too, images of the iron gauntlets which fitted over the wrists and could be tightened with screws, and of the awful rack.

This last instrument of torture was a wooden frame with rollers at each end. Ropes ran around the rollers and the ends of the ropes were fastened to the prisoner's wrists and ankles. Then, when the rollers were revolved, arms and legs were stretched, often so far that all the limbs became disjointed.

One of the cruelest of the rack-masters, as they

were called, was a man named Topcliffe. He per-
formed his horrible work some years after Father
Campion had met his Lord at Tyburn. He once
boasted, referring to another Jesuit he was going
to torture on the rack, that he would "make him
a foot taller than he was before".

Is it any wonder, then, that for Father Campion,
and for hundreds of others like him in those terrible
days, the Tower of London was not a pleasant or
a quaint place, but an abode of horrors? Is there
any wonder that he, known for his bravery and
his gallantry, now knelt in his dismal cell and repeated the prayer that our Lord had uttered to his
Father during his agony in the garden: "Not my
will but thine be done"?

Christ's hero did not have long to wait before
his worst anticipation began to come true. The
warden of the Tower was Sir Owen Hopton, who
was seeking advancement in the Queen's service.
As soon as he heard that the famous Campion,
the biggest prize yet to be caught, would be committed to his charge in the Tower, he thought,
"I'll show the Queen and Lord Leicester how zeal-
ous I can be in the performance of my duty. From
the very start I'll be as severe as I can with the
traitor, and when Her Majesty hears of it, she will
certainly give me a promotion."

At the very moment when Father Campion was
praying in his cell, Sir Owen was giving orders

to have Little Ease made ready for him. On the afternoon of July 22, the door of Father Campion's cell groaned open and a jailer's voice growled: "Come along, seditious Jesuit, we have a little surprise for you."

Father Campion blessed himself, rose, and followed down the gloomy corridors. Another door swung open and he saw before him the small room, absolutely bare and almost pitch dark, even with the door open, which he knew to be Little Ease. Sir Owen stood to one side, elegant and disdainful, watching the weary, disheveled man gaze in fascinated horror at the dreadful room.

"Well, then, Mr. Campion," he said mockingly, "where is all the bravery you protested in your lying *Brag*? If the sight of our Little Ease affrights you so much, how pale do you think your face will become when you see some of the other means we have here to break the spirit of rebellious citizens like you and your fellow priests?"

"Fear is not the same as cowardice, Sir Owen", responded Father Campion with a calm dignity, and a trace of his famous smile began to show on his haggard face. "I never said, nor could I, for I am a man, and not an angel, that I would not feel fear at what lies in store for me. But I did say, and with the grace of our Lord, I will prove it, that I would not be broken in spirit and betray either my Lord Christ or those Catholic friends who have sheltered me and to whom I have brought the holy Mass and the word of God."

"Humph! Well, we shall soon see. In with the man, and let him think over his deeds and his boasts for a while."

"By what right am I subjected to this torture?" cried Father Campion in a commanding voice. "I am an Englishman, I have not been tried, I have not yet been found guilty of any crime. Torture is for criminals—if indeed it is for anyone who is a human being. I demand to see the writ of the Privy Council which gives you the authority so to treat me."

"You can demand until you are blue in the face, my good papist", snarled Sir Owen. "I am master of this Tower, and who's to know that I have given you a little taste of discipline?" He nodded his head to one of the jailers. The man stepped behind Father Campion, grabbed him by the shoulders and pushed him, not too gently, into Little Ease. The door was slammed shut; the darkness closed in on the figure of Edmund Campion huddled in a cramped, bent-over, standing position.

For three full days and part of a fourth, Father Campion got to know the "little taste of discipline" Little Ease could administer. When his legs and back began to tremble and twitch from the strain of trying to stand, he would slump to a crowded sitting position, and when he could bear that no longer, he would struggle to stand again. Would

the hours never pass? How many hours had to
pass before he would either be released or lose con-
sciousness? And yet, he prayed not to lose con-
sciousness. He prayed that he might remain in control of his mind and will so that he could consciously
offer his suffering in reparation for his own sins
and for the conversion of his beloved England.

We do not know whether his prayer was granted.
But on the morning of July 25, the door of Little
Ease was flung open and Father Campion was commanded to come out. He thought he was going
to be led back to his cell. His amazement grew
and grew as he saw that he was being led to the
street entrance of the Tower. Could it be possible
that he was to be set free? He knew better than
to hope for that even in his wildest dreams; but
why was he being led outdoors?

A few more steps and the fresh air and the sunlight
nearly blinded him and made his head reel with
giddiness. When he came back to earth again, he
saw that he was surrounded by a heavy guard and
that they were standing on the steps of the Tower
that led down to the bank of the Thames River.
A boat was nearing the steps. When it had touched,
the guards, with Father Campion in their midst,
stepped in and the oarsmen pushed off and began
to row upstream. Not a word was spoken, and
Father Campion still did not have the faintest idea
of what it was all about.

Soon, however, he saw that they were heading

toward a large house he knew well. It was Leicester House, and in it lived Lord Leicester, the man who had once admired Edmund Campion and even been his patron. Now he was directing the pursuit that had tracked Father Campion down and was hot on the trail of all other priests in the realm, especially of the Jesuits—if indeed any more of them were at large.

Father Campion's heart leaped a bit. Perhaps, after all, Lord Leicester was relenting. Perhaps orders had come from the Queen herself that, since Father Campion had made it clear in his *Brag* that he was not a traitor, he might at least be set at liberty—if not to continue to work as a priest in England. But then his heart sank, for if he were released only to be banished from his native land, life for him would hardly be worth living. To bring England back to the old Faith was all his hope and all his ambition.

The boat touched the steps that led up to the broad terrace of Leicester House. Up the band climbed; in through the broad doors they went; through elegant rooms they passed, until they stood before a door guarded by two soldiers. The doors were thrown open; the guard around Father Campion stepped aside and back, and alone in the center of the doorway, he looked into a large room.

His eyes widened with amazement. On either side of a large and regal chair stood Lord Leicester, the Earl of Bedford, and two men he recognized as secretaries of state. This was amazing enough, but the wonder of wonders was that on the throne-like chair sat . . . Queen Elizabeth!

In the split second before he went down on one knee to the Queen, Father Campion, gazing on the towering red wig and the dead-white, powdered face, saw in his mind's eye the younger Queen Elizabeth before whom he had read his Latin greeting when she had visited Oxford University. How close they had been then; and how great was the difference between them now! Then he had been in her favor, had served at her Court, and had seemed likely to go far in positions of honor. Now he was a man who had been hunted down; now she was his enemy.

God knows that Father Campion did not want Queen Elizabeth, or any other person in the world, to be his enemy. His life—his vocation—was to bring the peace of Christ and of the Church to all men, and especially to those of his native land. He was not the Queen's enemy; he loved her for her soul's sake. But the Queen considered him her enemy and break his spirit she would, even if it meant forgetting all the pleasant memories she still had of the charming young man who had pleased her so much back in those days of her Oxford visit.

"My Queen", exclaimed Father Campion, on one knee and bowing his head.

"Rise, Mr. Campion."

How old and weary the voice sounds, thought Father Campion as he painfully rose, for the cramps from Little Ease still gripped and twisted his muscles.

"You said, 'My Queen', Mr. Campion", said the tired voice. "Do you say it from the heart, or is the sentiment another of the tricks of the popish priests and the Jesuits?"

"I cannot tell what is in the hearts of others, Your Majesty, but I do know what is in mine. And I protest that I do now recognize you, and always have, to be the Queen of England—and I am an Englishman."

"Then you and your companion Persons are not back to incite my subjects to rebellion?" queried the Queen.

"That Your Majesty must know from the statement I have made, which some men have called Campion's *Brag*."

"Humph! A most prideful document, I must say. But yes, I do know that you protest that you are back in England only for the spiritual benefit of those you can reach. I am inclined to believe you—that you have not meddled nor intend to meddle in affairs of state. But there is still something against you. You are a papist."

"Which is my greatest glory", proclaimed Father Campion, his head lifted proudly, his frank eyes gazing unafraid into the masklike countenance of the Queen.

By this time Lord Leicester and the Earl of Bedford were stirring a bit impatiently. Leicester bent over and whispered into the Queen's ear. She nodded and flicked him away with a motion of her hand.

"We are prepared, Mr. Campion," she said, as though offering a great favor, "we are prepared to advance you in the service of the Church of England if you will make a public declaration that you have abandoned the Church of Rome. There may be no limit to the honors that may come to you if you will renounce the Pope and all he stands for. Give it careful thought, Mr. Campion, for the choice before you is either honors or death."

There was a deadly silence in the room—for the space of a few seconds only. Then the Queen and her advisers heard the most unlikely sound—the sound of laughter. It was not loud, but a sort of deep chuckle that welled up from the heart and soul of Father Campion. It was the laughter of a Christian man who knew that he had won. At last he had it from their own lips—he was to be put to death solely because he was a Catholic and a priest. Politics had nothing to do with what they thought of him. The people of England at the time might think that he was going to his death because he was a traitor, but those who were to send him to Tyburn had declared that he was to die for his Faith. One day the whole world would know the truth. He had won!

"Your Majesty," said Father Campion in a grave tone, "for the past ten years I have given this matter thought. I thought about it seriously when I left the Church of England and went to the Continent to be reconciled to Rome. I thought of it seriously when I entered the Society of Jesus and was ordained a priest. And ever since I have been back in England, how many times have I thought that I could indeed save my life if I turned traitor to my Lord Christ and his Church! But he himself has said to us all: 'He who would save his life must lose it.'

"I remain true to Christ and his Church", he ended in a loud and triumphant voice.

There was another dead silence—this time for more than a few seconds. The Queen and her councillors stared—it seemed even with admiration—at this handsome, talented, brave young man, who had the world at his feet and preferred the horrors of the Tower and Tyburn.

The Queen sighed, waved her hand. The doors opened; the prison guard waited to surround Father Campion and lead him back to the Tower.

Five days later, Sir Owen Hopton opened a letter from the Queen's Council. It was an order to start the process of torture by which it was hoped to break the hero's spirit.

11

TRIAL AND CONDEMNATION

I NSIDE THE GLOOMY WALLS of the Tower of London
there is a chapel. In the day of our story, it
was used sometimes for services, but more often
as an examination room to which prisoners were
taken for questioning before they went to the formal
trial.

The stained-glass windows still had the glory
that was burned into them when the chapel was
built for the glory of God. But the light that
streamed through those windows had, in the years
since King Henry set himself up in opposition to
the Pope, lit up many a scene that had dishonored
God's mercy and justice.

It is doubtful whether the chapel, in all its history, ever saw such a mockery of justice as took place within its walls when Father Campion was four times examined in an attempt to get him to confess that he was a traitor to the Queen.

The first "conference" took place on September 1. Father Campion had returned to his prison cell, after refusing the Queen's offer, on July 25. During the month he had been tortured on the rack four times. What were his jailers trying to get from the broken body? They were trying to get him to tell the names of all those in whose homes he had said Mass, the names of those he had reconciled to the Faith.

Meanwhile, the Queen's agents were spreading rumors up and down the land. Campion had confessed! Campion was going to appear in public and announce that he had accepted the Protestant religion! Campion had betrayed his friends! The circulation of these rumors was supposed to dishearten the Catholics, to show them that their beloved leader had played them false; and so, perhaps, many another Catholic would give in and deny his Faith.

There was, to be sure, confusion among the Catholics, because not one word could possibly be gotten to them from Father Campion himself. He was as if dead for the month—dead and buried in his cell after the horrible tortures that he had undergone.

But he had revealed nothing. His jailers made up lists of names and released them as ones that Father Campion had revealed. It is certain, though, that the brave priest did not tell anything that would put anyone else in danger.

The morning of September 1 came. There was a great bustling and preparation in the Tower, but Father Campion, almost unconscious in his cell, heard nothing but the echo in his mind of the creaking of the ropes of the rack, as they tightened and tightened and stretched and stretched his limbs until they started from their sockets.

The bustle ceased and there was an air of expectancy in the Tower. Father Campion's cell was flung open, the fetters were removed, and he was commanded to follow. He tottered to his feet, sprawled and fell, rose again, and stumbled on his nerveless legs after his guide. Outside the door of the prison chapel he saw and recognized other priests and some Catholic prisoners. The chapel doors swung back, and Father Campion and his companions entered the chapel for the first of their "examinations".

On one side of the chapel a sort of grandstand had been erected. In it sat members of the Court and of the Privy Council, there to see the sport. On the other side sat two Protestant clergymen who were to be the examiners. Witnesses were ready in another part of the chapel, and guards kept watch. A good crowd of curious spectators filled the remaining space.

Father Campion was made to sit on a little stool, without any support for his broken body. There was no desk before him, with paper and pens and reference books. He was alone, helpless, save for his valiant soul and his quick mind—but could it be quick after the tortures he had suffered?

The examiners were surrounded by clerks who, in turn, were surrounded by books and documents. If a question were to arise about what the Scriptures said, Father Campion would have to quote from memory, and give chapter and verse, too, out of his poor aching head.

His examiners, however, could turn to the clerks and have the passage pointed out for them to read aloud. The purpose of this uneven contest was to try first to get Father Campion to admit that the Catholic Faith was wrong; second, to make him look foolish in the eyes of his fellow Catholics, who not only revered him as a priest, but admired him as a scholar.

The questioning and answering went on all the long day. Often Father Campion reeled on his little stool and had to be propped up again while the questions rang and clanged in his head.

Once he was asked to prove his point by quoting a passage from the Scriptures in the original Greek.

He started, but he could not remember the rest of the text.

"So," crowed one of the examiners, "this is the famous scholar who wrote the boastful *Brag* and the most learned *Ten Reasons*! Why, the man is no scholar at all, and even his Greek accent is that of a barbarian. That comes, I suppose, from having studied in Rome."

There was a burst of mocking laughter from some of the spectators, but one could see on the faces of others a look of utter disgust at this unfair treatment.

"My Lord," Father Campion managed to pant, "it is not a question of whether or not I am a scholar. It is whether the doctrine of the Church of Rome is the doctrine of Jesus Christ. On that alone am I being examined."

"Do you mean to say, Campion," thundered his Lordship, "that you are not getting a fair trial here?"

"Fair trial?" cried Father Campion. "It is a trial to shame every Englishman in the land. You put me to the rack first; then you take from me all my books and papers; you prepare your questions for days and weeks, and I am dragged in to answer without a moment's preparation. I call upon God and upon all Englishmen here present and throughout the land to witness if this is a fair trial."

"Your sessions on the rack, Campion," replied the judge, "have nothing to do with these examinations. You were racked because you are a traitor. You are here being questioned on matters of religion."

At this, Father Campion leaped as fast as he could to his crippled feet and cried in a loud voice:

"If any of you can prove me guilty of any crime except my religion, I will willingly agree to suffer the extremest torments you can inflict."

Even in that hostile room a hush settled down, and from the ranks of the Court people a little cry of "well spoken" was heard. Heads turned and young Philip, Earl of Arundel, blushed and hung his head. But from that moment he knew, as he later said, "on which side the truth and true religion were". He gave up his life of pleasure and extravagance and became a Roman Catholic.

The first examination ended. Father Campion was led back to his cell, where he remained, more dead than alive, for eighteen days. When the door at last opened once again and he was led to the second conference, he thought only a week had passed. Though so shattered in body and so blurred in thought, never, in all these terrible days, did he show that his mind was hazy in matters of faith and his Catholic and priestly life.

The second examination followed the pattern of

the first. Theological questions that were deep and complex were hurled at his head. As usual, he had only his memory and his native intelligence to depend on while his adversaries had books and assistant clerks. This time the conference was held in a smaller hall so that the public could be excluded. Father Campion's judges did not want to have another outbreak of applause for the "traitor" to embarrass them again.

A third and a fourth examination were held on September 23 and 27; and at the end of the four unjust sessions, Father Campion, more and more broken in body, had more than held his own with his adversaries.

News of this leaked out even into the streets, and many of the people began to jeer openly at the mockery of the "discussions" to which he had been subjected. Ballads were being sung in the byways of London, in which Campion was called "champion", and in which it was said that Campion was being dealt with "by the rack instead of good government".

This state of affairs could not be allowed to go on, so the Privy Council determined to put an end to the theological disputations and to hurry on to the public trial. Trial? It could be nothing like a trial, because Father Campion had already been judged and sentenced in the hearts and minds of his captors. They would go through the motions, but it was clear that, from the moment Eliot had pried open the hiding place at Lyford Grange, Father Campion had already been doomed to the gallows at Tyburn.

On November 14 Father Campion stood before the bar in Westminster Hall. He could barely remain upright, but when he heard the charge against him, he raised his head and cried in an indignant voice:

"I protest before God and his holy angels, before heaven and earth, before the world and the bar before which I stand, which is but a small resemblance of the terrible judgment of the next life, that I am not guilty of any part of the treason contained in the indictment, or of any other treason whatever."

And well he might protest, for he was being charged with the very things the Queen and her ministers had said they did not believe him guilty of. But he had to be put to death—and for being a traitor. If he were put to death merely for being a papist and a priest, the public would consider him a martyr. That would not do, for then the Catholics would be strengthened in their Faith. Campion had to be discredited and made to look like a faithless Englishman.

The judge who had read the charge looked down his nose at Father Campion.

"The trial will soon begin and you will have

full justice, Campion", he drawled. "Now all we want to know is: Do you plead guilty or not guilty, and take care, for you must swear to the truth of your answer."

"I plead not guilty."

"Then raise your hand and take the oath."

Father Campion removed his right hand from the sleeve of his coat where he had been hiding it, for it was numb and twisted. He tried to raise it. He could not. One of his fellow prisoners stepped over, took Father Campion's hand in his own, bent over and kissed the tortured palm, and raised Father Campion's hand for him.

The day—November 20. The hall at Westminster was crowded. The judges were all in place. Guards were posted, the lawyers assembled. Only the Crown had lawyers; the accused were not allowed to have any.

It was a lively assembly. The members of Court were in their fine clothes, the judges in their gowns, the soldiers in their uniforms.

The doors in the back of the hall opened and Father Campion was led in.

"Campion," intoned the judge, "you pleaded not guilty on November 14 to the charge against you. I will read that charge again, and we shall then proceed to the trial.

"The charge is that you plotted in Rome on

March 31 of the preceding year to start a conspiracy to murder the Queen; that, on May 20, you and others exhorted foreigners to invade this country; that you have been sent to England to stir up unrest to make the country ready for rebellion.

"This is the charge to which you have pleaded not guilty. We shall now proceed to call witnesses."

Witnesses? Who were called? Eliot, for one, and others like him. We know their names and their background. The others were named Sledd, Munday, and Caddy. Each of these men swore that the priests now in England and now on trial with Father Campion had told them about this plot. The priests, with Father Campion as their spokesman, denied it—and that was the end of the trial.

Father Campion could call no one to witness for him. It was his word against the word of men who were known to be paid informers—and worse.

When the testimony was all in, and Father Campion was given a chance to have a small say, he exclaimed:

"What truths can you expect from their mouths? One has confessed himself a murderer, the other a destestable atheist, a profane heathen, a destroyer of two men already. On your consciences, would you believe them—they that have betrayed both God and man, nay, that have nothing left to swear by, neither religion nor honesty? Even if you would believe them, can you? I commit the rest to God, and our convictions to your good discretions."

The judges listened with unmoved faces. The chief judge nodded to the jury. They rose and went into a side room. There was now a long pause. Father Campion sat on his little stool, his head bent, his lips moving in prayer, a look of great peace on his face.

"He certainly does not look like a traitor", whispered more than one among the spectators.

"He isn't", another would whisper back, looking over his shoulder to be sure he was not being overheard. "He's going to the joys of Tyburn just because he is a Catholic and a priest . . . but don't dare ever say that I said that . . ."

The door of the jury room opened. The jury tramped back.

"What is your verdict?"

"We find the defendant, Edmund Campion, guilty as charged."

The heavy features of the chief judge turned to Campion.

"Campion and the rest," he said, "what can you say? Why should you not die?"

With a face that glowed with nobility and dignity and with a strange inner joy that amazed the spectators, Edmund Campion—Catholic, Jesuit, priest, Englishman—replied in tones to thrill all good men everywhere and all good Englishmen of his own times and all times:

"The only thing I have now to say is, that if my religion makes me a traitor, I am worthy to be condemned. Otherwise I am, and have been, as good a subject as ever the Queen had.

"In condemning me you condemn all your own ancestors—all the ancient priests, bishops, and kings—all that was once the glory of England, the island of saints, and the most devoted child of the See of Peter.

"For what have I taught . . . that they did not teach? To be condemned with these lights—not of England only, but of the world—by their degenerate descendants, is both gladness and joy.

"God lives; posterity will live; their judgment is not so liable to corruption as that of those who are now going to sentence me to death."

And the sentence came as soon as Father Campion finished his glorious testimony. Without letting a muscle of his impassive face move at the words of Father Campion, the judge put his black cap on his head, picked up a paper, and read from it:

"You must go to the place from which you came, there to remain until you will be drawn through the open City of London upon hurdles to the place of execution, and there be hanged and let down alive, and your entrails be taken out and burnt in your sight; then your head to be cut off and your body to be divided into four parts, to be disposed of at Her Majesty's pleasure. And may God have mercy on your soul."

Through the silence that followed this dreadful

sentence, there rose the sound of a voice still young, though strained with suffering and utter weariness. The voice, pouring out from a countenance that glowed with triumph, sang. It sang *Te Deum lauda-mus*—we praise you, O God.

12

THE JEWEL MERCHANT WINS
THE GREATEST JEWEL

FOR ELEVEN DAYS after the "trial", Father Campion lay in his dark prison cell with iron fetters on his hands and feet. Visions of the horrible fate that was in store for him rose from time to time before his eyes, and then it was that he repeated over and over the words of his Lord, "Not my will but thine be done."

There is not much on record about the visitors he had during these lonely days. It seems that his sister—about whom little is known—came to see him and to press him to accept the Queen's pardon if he would renounce his Catholic Faith.

One day the most wonderful visit of all took place. The doors of Father Campion's gloomy cell swung back. As he looked up, squinting at the unaccustomed light, he saw, standing in the corridor behind the guard, George Eliot—the man who had tracked him down and brought him to this terrible and glorious end.

"Go on in, Eliot", the guard said. Eliot hesitated a bit, shrugged his shoulders, and stepped into the cell. Father Campion raised his manacled hands as far as he could in greeting and managed to croak in a weary, weary voice:

"Welcome, Mr. Eliot. I am sorry that I cannot rise to greet you, but you see that traitors must be dealt with very cautiously."

His haggard face crinkled with his famous smile, and Eliot lowered his gaze.

"Mr. Campion," he stammered, "if I had thought that you would have to suffer anything more than imprisonment because of my accusations, I would never have turned you in, no matter what I might have lost of the Queen's favor."

Father Campion looked long at the infamous man. Could this be true? Could Eliot be sincere? It was not for Father Campion to judge, and so, with a sigh, he answered:

"If that is the case, I beseech you, in God's name, to do penance, and confess your crime, to God's glory and your own salvation."

Eliot stared. Perhaps it was on the tip of his conscience to yield and admit his evildoing. Certainly the love and charity that shone on the haggard face of Father Campion were enough to move any man to fling himself at the priest's feet and beg forgiveness.

But another thought was uppermost in Eliot's mind. He knew full well the black looks he was getting from all sides. Even those who had no love for the Church and the Pope still felt that Eliot had done a most detestable deed in bearing false witness against Father Campion at the trial. Eliot, in short, was fearful for his life. He could not bear the thought that he would have to live the rest of his days in fear that he would be killed by someone who revered Father Campion.

Cringing and stammering, Eliot told Father Campion of this fear.

Father Campion, with a prayer in his heart that Eliot would begin to think of his sins rather than of his physical safety, replied:

"My good Eliot, how little you know what Catholics are, though you have professed to be one. I know that many are calling you a Judas, but you are much deceived if you think that Catholics push their detestation and wrath as far as revenge. Yet, if you would feel quite safe, I will recommend you to a Catholic duke I know in Germany. Under his protection you will be able to live in perfect security. There is not much time left to me, but I will get a letter off to the duke, if you so will."

Eliot shifted from foot to foot, evaded the frank gaze of Father Campion, and finally muttered something about wanting to think it over. He did think it over, and the result was that he went back to his slimy business of spying. We lose sight of Eliot here, but there was one result of the interview he had with Father Campion.

The jailer who had charge of Father Campion at this time was a man named Delahays. He had listened in on the exchange between Father Campion and Eliot and was so impressed with Father Campion's kindness and charity that he became a Catholic. So, even in irons, Father Campion continued his work of bringing souls back to Christ.

His own soul was soon to meet his Master, Christ. This thought sustained him in all the dark and cheerless days until the dawn of December 1, 1581. On that morning, Father Campion was led out of his cell. He was kept waiting for some hours while a search was made for the clothes he had worn when arrested. The Council thought that if they dressed Father Campion in the clothes he had worn while traveling in disguise, this would make him look more ridiculous. He would look like the traitor they were proclaiming he was. But the clothes could not be found, so a jailer threw at him the loose, sacklike gown he had worn in prison.

"Put this on, traitor", he growled. "You won't have to wear it very long."

"Thank you", said Father Campion. "I trust that, in God's good pleasure, I may soon exchange it for another garment which he will vest me with."

"It will be a bloody garment, Mr. Campion", the jailer chuckled meanly.

"Yes, I know. But it will be, in God's time and grace, the salvation of England."

"England, England", sneered the jailer. "What do you or those like you care for England?"

"Much, much more than you think", replied Father Campion in a low and intense voice. "We care for it as Christ does. He died and yet lives; we die and yet England will live because of those she thus puts to death. Live England! Live the Queen! But above all, live Christ in the hearts and souls of Englishmen!"

The jailer gaped in amazement. How did such ringing tones come from a body that had been racked and broken? It seemed to him that he heard from the mouth of a condemned man a chant that told of victory—a triumphal shout. Could it be that this Mr. Campion was really the winner? Could it be that the Queen and all her counselors had really lost?

The jailer felt a little shiver run up and down his back. He didn't hold with the popish doctrine about saints, but it certainly seemed to him that this Mr. Campion was about the nearest thing to a saint he would ever meet.

"Anyway," he muttered, to hide his real feelings, "give me your pardon if I have treated you amiss."

Father Campion's face lit up. "With all my heart do I pardon you. I will remember you to my Lord Christ. Do you, too, pray for me."

London was a sea of mud. It had been raining for days, and the narrow streets were ankle-deep in muck. But there was a festive air in the crowds that were assembled. As the door of the Tower was opened and Father Campion was led out, a great cry arose from the crowd that had gathered about the prison. Was it a cry of greeting—or a cry of hatred? One could hardly tell.

Mingled emotions welled up in the shout. Some were there to tell Father Campion by their presence that they had taken new heart because of him. Others really felt that they were there to see justice done to a traitor. But one mystery was solved for all—for those who were for Father Campion and those who were against him. Here he was.

Rumors had spread among the people that Father Campion had committed suicide in prison; that Father Campion had given in and renounced his Faith; that Father Campion had been spirited away across the Channel; that Father Campion would never come to the last extremity of his execution.

But here was Father Campion, and the populace would have the pleasure of seeing him mount the steps of Tyburn and pay the last farthing of his devotion.

Before the doors of the Tower a horse was waiting. Attached to the beast was a hurdle. It looked something like a carpenter's "horse". To this Father Campion was tied, and the last journey started. Dragged along on the hurdle, Father Campion was soon a mass of mud and filth, but every now and again some kind soul in the crowd would push forward and wipe the mire from his face.

"God bless and love you", Father Campion would murmur, and in his mind would rise thoughts of our Lord on his way to Calvary and of Veronica braving the jeers of the crowd to wipe the Holy Face.

The way to Tyburn went by a place called Newgate Arch. There, in a niche, still stood a statue of the Blessed Virgin. Through the mud that caked his face and blurred his vision, Father Campion saw the statue and tried to raise his bound hands in salute.

With this, a loud laugh welled up in the crowd, but Father Campion only smiled to himself and to his Lady and murmured: "God make you all good Catholics."

Plod, plod went the horse. Bump, bump went Father Campion behind. Was this the glorious death for Christ that Father Campion had lived so often in thought? What was glorious about it? It was all a matter of mud and filth and jeering crowds and a Protestant minister plodding at Father Campion's heels, exhorting him to see the "truth" at last and renounce the Pope of Rome.

Yet, thought Father Campion, the Way of the Cross of Christ was not glamorous, either. That, too, had been humiliating and dirty and common. If Christ's death had redeemed the world, thought Father Campion, my own death may, in union with my Lord's, be a way to save my dear England.

The plodding horse stopped at Tyburn. Father Campion was untied. He stood there, looking out and around. Before him was an immense crowd. The ordinary people stood at the foot of the gallows. Off a little way was a grandstand, and in it, dressed in all their finery, sat members of the court and of the nobility.

Public executions in those days were a matter of sport, and it was quite the thing for gentlemen and ladies, who would be very kind to their own children, to assemble in a mood of pleasant excitement to witness the brutal death of a criminal. And no criminal could provide more entertainment than a condemned papist.

Father Campion did not know it, but in the crowd thronging at the foot of the gallows was young

William Harrington. Since the day he had fled from Lyford Grange, William had been following the fate of his beloved Father Campion. He had heard from a Catholic man who had been present at the trial how Father Campion had won the day by his calm and dignity. He had heard whispered and hinted how the brave priest had withstood the torture of the rack. Now, though he knew there was nothing he could do save pray, he stood, jostled and pushed about by the crowd, looking up at the figure of his dear Father Campion.

"Oh," he thought, "if there were only something I could do. If only I could tell this mob of people how brave and gentle and truly English Father Campion is. But no—that is not the way it has to be. Dear Father Campion will go to his death, and few will now know what it is he is doing. I do know, please God, and with his help, I will follow Father Campion in God's good time."

William pushed nearer the high platform on which stood the menacing gallows. He stared at the cross-shaped structure, and a shiver ran up and down his spine.

Through the crowds and over the roar of shouts and rowdy laughter, William saw Father Campion stand up after he had been untied from the hurdle. Then he was pushed and bustled onto a cart underneath the gallows. The noose was fitted over his head. The supreme moment Father Campion had been looking forward to for years was at hand; he was to lay down his life for Christ and his Church.

But there was a pause. Some of the members of the Queen's Council and some Protestant ministers crowded about Father Campion. Here they, too, had their last chance. Perhaps Father Campion could be persuaded at the very end to confess his "crimes". William's heart beat fast as he stood close and listened.

"Confess your treason, Campion", shouted one of the Queen's councillors. "This is the last chance you will have to admit that you have been a false subject to Her Majesty."

"As to the treasons that have been laid at my door," replied Father Campion in a strong voice, "and for which I am come here to suffer, I desire you all to bear witness with me that I am thereof altogether innocent."

"Oh, no, Campion," cried another of the nobles, "it is too late now to deny what was proved against you in open court."

"Proved?" cried Father Campion. "What was proved was simply that I am a Catholic man and a priest; in that Faith have I lived and in that Faith I intend to die. If you esteem my religion treason, then I am guilty; as for the other treason, I never committed any, God is my judge. But you have now what you desire. I beseech you to have patience, and suffer me to speak a word or two for the discharge of my conscience."

But the babel of voices swelled and roared around the muddy and broken figure. William, listening with all his heart, heard the voice of Father Campion above the din. And what he heard made tears of joy and love start up in his eyes, for Father Campion was praying for those who had brought him to this awful end. He asked God to forgive all who had borne false witness against him; he forgave the jury and the very man who was to butcher him to death. Then he ceased, save that his lips continued to move in silent prayer.

The senseless debate was not yet over. A minister stepped forward and tried to lead Father Campion in prayer. Father Campion looked up at him gently and said:

"Sir, you and I are not one in religion, wherefore I pray you content yourself. I bar none of prayer; but I only desire them that are of the household of the Faith to pray with me, and in my agony to say one creed."

"But why do you insist on praying in Latin? Pray in English like any good Englishman."

"Do you mind?" replied Father Campion with great mildness. "I will pray to God in a language we both well understand."

"But at least admit your crimes against the Queen

and beg her forgiveness, Campion", thundered one of the Council.

"Wherein have I offended her? In this I am innocent. This is my last speech; in this give me credit—I have and do pray for her."

"You pray for the Queen, you say. But what Queen is it you pray for, traitor?"

"I pray for Elizabeth, your Queen and my Queen, unto whom I wish a long quiet reign with all prosperity."

These were Father Campion's last words. Young William Harrington turned his head away as the driver of the cart raised his whip and brought it down smartly on the horse's back. The horse bolted forward. The cart was swept away from under Father Campion's feet, the rope tightened, the noose closed, and there, against the gloomy and stormy sky of London, a dirty and twitching figure swung in the death agony. In a few moments the body was cut down and the rest of the horrible sentence was carried out.

William Harrington felt as though his heart would burst. What was it he felt? Was it sorrow, or joy, or horror at the butchery? It was hard to tell right then, but years later he would know what the emotion was, for he, too, would follow the footsteps of his beloved Father Campion—and they would be footsteps that led to glory, no matter how brutal and inhuman the execution that would lead to that glory.

There was a moment's silence all over the large crowd. Here and there voices could be heard raised in the prayer Father Campion had asked for. There was the sound of intaken breath from the mob. Lungs were filled with the murky London air, and then, an explosion of sound—cheering, cries of mockery, crude laughter, all drowning out the sound of the executioner's ax.

In her apartments, the Queen had been pacing back and forward. Early that morning it would not have been too late to cancel the execution. Should she call it off? But no, it was too late. Now that Campion had been condemned for treason, the Queen could not free him. She knew, though, as she had admitted, that she had no more loyal subject than the young man to whom she had been so attracted many years ago.

She sat and began playing with letters before her on the desk. An attendant waited. The Queen turned impatiently:

"Has the execution taken place yet?" she croaked.

"No, Your Majesty, but I fancy that when it does we shall be able to know the exact moment, for there is certain to be a great roar from the crowd when the traitor Campion gets what he deserves."

"Keep your opinions to yourself, hussy", barked the Queen. "Traitor, indeed! I would that all my ministers were as loyal."

The attendant gaped in surprise, but at this instant, through the open windows came a great, animal-like roar.

The Queen hurried to a window. Could it be that she saw the glint of steel in the distance as the ax rose and fell and rose and fell again? She shuddered a little and turned away.

Had the attendant been near enough, she might have heard the Queen heave a deep sigh and mutter to herself:

"The flower of the realm! Where will it all end if I have to put such men to death? Who will be left? Who will love England for its own sake and not for the favors they hope to have from me? God save England and give me back noble men to help me."

But England was saved—in a higher sense than the Queen ever meant. It was, in God's Providence, saved by men like Father Campion and the hundreds who followed him up the bloody path of martyrdom. The Catholic strength of England, strong today and growing, took its nourishment from the blood of the martyrs. It has always been thus. Father Campion had foretold it. His dismembered body at Tyburn proclaimed it to the world. What was it he had written in his famous *Brag*?

Be it known to you that we have made a league—
all the Jesuits in the world . . . —cheerfully to
carry the cross you shall lay upon us, and never
to despair your recovery, while we have a man
left to enjoy your Tyburn, or to be racked with
your torments, or consumed with your prisons.
The expense is reckoned, the enterprise is begun;
it is of God, it cannot be withstood. So the faith
was planted: so it must be restored.

13

AFTERWARD

THE HOWLING OF THE MOB grew less and less. After Father Campion, two other heroes suffered the same fate; but the curiosity of the crowd had been satisfied when Father Campion paid the final penalty for his devotion to Christ and his Church. Little by little the crowd dispersed. The nobles, tired of the sport, stepped down from the grandstand, and the rest of the executions went ahead with relatively few spectators.

Young William Harrington tore his eyes away from the grim gallows of Tyburn. He heaved a great sigh from the bottom of his heart. He felt within himself a sense of great peace, and even of love, for all the poor deluded people who had come to see the death of the "traitor".

"Please God," he said to himself, "and in his good time, all the world will come to know what a brave and gracious Englishman has here today given all he had to give. May I, too, be as generous one of these days."

At this very moment, another young man, not too far from William at the terrible scene, was staring down at the sleeve of his jacket as though seeing a miracle or a nightmare.

Henry Walpole was a young man who had quite a reputation for being a wit, a young poet, a fashion plate. He knew all the best people, and if this led him to play down his Catholicism, well, who would know too much about it? He was a Catholic, but one had to get along, didn't one? And so he was not too faithful about attending Mass and frequenting the sacraments.

Walpole was one of the Catholics of the time who coasted with the decisions of the Queen and her Council. He was one of the Catholics to whom Father Campion's mission had been a challenge and a dare. Many Catholic families like the Walpoles had caught fire from the preaching and example of Father Campion and had returned to a fervent practice of their Faith.

Henry Walpole, though he had heard about Father Campion and admired him from afar, was not too interested in taking chances. Why should he trouble himself with theological matters, and perhaps lose the favor of those at Court, by being too devout a Catholic?

Moved more by curiosity than by faith, he had come to the execution. After all, many of his friends were there, and it would do him little harm if he were seen there to witness the death of a traitor. He had edged his way up close to the gallows. He had stared partly in revulsion, partly in fascination as the bloody business of the execution went on.

But all of a sudden he gave a great start. He flinched and turned pale. He stared at the sleeve of his jacket. On it was a great blob of blood. It had splashed down from the platform when the executioner wielded his ax. It was, Henry knew, the blood of a priest-martyr. It was the blood of one who had been ready and eager to give all for his Lord Christ.

As Henry stared at the blotch on his sleeve, it seemed to him that he heard a voice saying, "And what are you, Henry, willing to give me?"

Henry reeled. He felt that he had been struck on the head. He staggered away from the scene of the execution. He went home. He changed not only his fine clothes, but his way of life as well.

In 1584 Walpole crossed the Channel to the Continent, was ordained a Jesuit, and returned to England on December 4, 1593. In less than twenty-four hours he was tracked down and sent to the Tower.

For a whole year he experienced the same fate as Father Campion. He was racked and tortured and tried, and on April 7, 1595, was hanged, drawn, and quartered at York. Father Campion had led him along the bloody, cruel, but glorious, way he had not dreamed of following when, out of vanity and curiosity, he had gone to witness the execution at Tyburn in 1581.

And what of William Harrington? After the execution of his hero, he went home to Mount Saint John. Some days later, he went to his father and said, in a low, calm voice:

"Father, you know what an impression Father Campion made when he was here. We were all convinced that he was a saint. I spoke to him then about going over to the Continent and becoming a priest. He thought then that perhaps John Yate and I had a vocation. I know now that I do have one.

"From the day I saw him go so gallantly to his death, I have felt deep in my heart that I am called to follow Father Campion—perhaps, if it be God's will, even to Tyburn. May I have your permission to go on to prepare for the priesthood?"

His father gave his son a long, loving look.

"You have counted what the cost may be, son?"

"Yes, father, I have. All I can now say is that I will prepare well. What God may ask me to do later for his Church and for England, only he knows."

"Kneel down, son, and I will give you my blessing. Then go and tell your mother. We will miss you sorely, but it is only by such sacrifices as we and you may be called on to make that the Faith will be restored to England."

The boy knelt, signed himself, rose, and took his leave of home and country.

In 1584 he went to Rheims. There he was ordained. He returned to England in 1592. After just about as long a time as Father Campion had spent on the mission in England, William Harrington was captured. He went to martyrdom at Tyburn on February 18, 1594.

When William Harrington stood underneath the gallows on that day, perhaps his thoughts reverted to the happy day at Mount Saint John when he had said to Father Campion:

"I think, Father, if the day comes for me to give all to Christ, I will be able to do it—because I have met you."

Certainly on the day of Father William's execution, they met.

And what, may we suppose, did they say to one another?

Who knows? But this they must have thought. It is in the words of gallant, brave, joyful Father Campion. It expresses the great and triumphant hope that England will still come back to the unity of the Catholic Church. Father Campion had said it; it is still the song of victory, not only for England, but for all the world:

> There will never want in England men that will have care for their own salvation, nor such as will advance other men's; neither shall this Church here ever fail so long as priests and pastors shall be found for their sheep . . .

Evelyn Waugh, in his life of Campion, has summed this all up in lovely words, with which we may end this version of a priest-hero's life:

> And so the work of Campion continued; so it continues. He was one of a host of martyrs, each, in their several ways, gallant and venerable; some performed more sensational feats of adventure, some sacrificed more conspicuous positions in the world, many suffered crueller tortures, but to his own, and to each succeeding generation, Campion's fame has burned with unique warmth and brilliance; it was his genius to express, in sentences that have resounded across the centuries, the spirit of chivalry in which they suffered, to typify in his zeal, his innocence, his inflexible purpose, the pattern which they followed. . . . We are the heirs of their conquest, and enjoy, at our ease, the plenty which they died to win.

APPENDIX

CAMPION'S BRAG

(To the Right Honorable, the Lords of Her Majesty's Privy Council)

Right Honorable:

Whereas I have come out of Germany and Bohemia, being sent by my Superiors, and adventured myself into this noble realm, my dear country, for the glory of God and benefit of souls, I thought it like enough that, in this busy, watchful and suspicious world, I should either sooner or later be intercepted and stopped of my course. Wherefore, providing for all events, and uncertain what may become of me, when God shall haply deliver my body into durance, I supposed it needful to put this writing in a readiness, desiring your good Lordships to give it your reading, for to know my cause. This doing, I trust I shall ease you of some labour. For that which otherwise you must have sought for by practice of wit, I do now lay into your hands by plain confession. And to the intent that the whole matter may be conceived in order, and so the better both understood and remembered, I make thereof these . . . points or articles, directly, truly and resolutely opening my full enterprise and purpose.

i. I confess that I am (albeit unworthy) a priest of the Catholic Church, and through the great mercy of God vowed now these eight years into the Order of the Society of Jesus. Hereby I have taken upon me a special kind of warfare under the banner of obedience, and even resigned all my interest or possibility of wealth, honor, pleasure and other worldly felicities.

ii. At the voice of our General Provost, which is to be a warrant from heaven, and Oracle of Christ, I took my voyage from Prague to Rome (where our said General Father is always resident) and from Rome to England, as I might and would have done joyously into any part of Christendome or Heathenesse, had I been thereto assigned.

iii. My charge is, of free cost to preach the Gospel, to minister the Sacraments, to instruct the simple, to reform sinners, to confute errors—in brief, to cry alarm spiritual against foul vice and proud ignorance, wherewith many of my dear countrymen are abused.

iv. I never had mind, and am strictly forbidden by our Father that sent me, to deal in any respect with matter of state or policy of this realm, as things which appertain not to my vocation, and from which I do gladly restrain and sequester my thoughts.

v. I do ask, to the glory of God, with all humility, and under your correction, three sorts of indifferent and quiet audiences: *the first* before your Honors, wherein I will discourse of religion, so far as it touches the commonweal and your nobilities: *the second*, whereof I make more account, before the Doctors and Masters and chosen men of both universities, wherein I undertake to avow the faith of our Catholic Church by proofs innumerable, Scriptures, councils, Fathers, history, natural and moral reasons: *the third* before the lawyers, spiritual and temporal, wherein I will justify the said faith by the common wisdom of the laws standing yet in force and practice.

vi. I would be loath to speak of anything that might sound of any insolent brag or challenge, especially being now as a dead man to this world and willing to put my head under every man's foot, and to kiss the ground they tread upon. Yet have

I such a courage in avouching the Majesty of Jesus my King, and such affiance in his gracious favor, and such assurance in my quarrel, and my evidence so impregnable, and because I know perfectly that no one Protestant, nor all the Protestants living, nor any sect of our adversaries (howsoever they face men down in pulpits, and overrule us in their kingdom of grammarians and unlearned ears) can maintain their doctrine in disputation. I am to sue most humble and instantly for the combat with all and every of them, and the most principal that may be found: protesting that in this trial the better furnished they come, the better welcome they shall be.

vii. And because it hath pleased God to enrich the Queen my Sovereign Lady with notable gifts of nature, learning, and princely education, I do verily trust that—if her Highness would vouchsafe her royal person and good attention to such a conference as, in the second part of my fifth article I have motioned, or to a few sermons, which in her or your hearing I am to utter,—such manifest and fair light by good method and plain dealing may be cast upon these controversies, that possibly her zeal of truth and love of her people shall incline her noble Grace to disfavor some proceedings hurtful to the realm, and procure towards us oppressed more equity.

viii. Moreover I doubt not but you her Highness'

Council being of such wisdom and discreet in cases most important, when you shall have heard these questions of religion opened faithfully, which many times by our adversaries are huddled up and confounded, will see upon what substantial grounds our Catholic Faith is built, how feeble that side is which by sway of the time prevails against us, and so at last for your own souls, and for many thousand souls that depend upon your government, will discountenance error when it is bewrayed, and hearken to those who would spend the best blood in their bodies for your salvation. Many innocent hands are lifted up to heaven for you daily by those English students, whose posterity shall never die, which beyond seas, gathering virtue and sufficient knowledge for the purpose, are determined never to give you over, but either to win you heaven, or to die upon your pikes. And touching our Society, be it known to you that we have made a league—the Jesuits in the world, whose succession and multitude must overreach all the practices of England—cheerfully to carry the cross you shall lay upon us, and never to despair your recovery, while we have a man left to enjoy your Tyburn, or to be racked with your torments, or consumed with your prisons. The expense is reckoned, the enterprise is begun; it is of God, it cannot be withstood. So the faith was planted: so it must be restored.

ix. If these my offers be refused, and my endeavors can take no place, and I, having run thousands of miles to do you good, shall be rewarded with rigor, I have no more to say but to recommend your case and mine to Almighty God, the Searcher of Hearts, who send us His grace, and set us at accord before the day of payment, to the end we may at last be friends in heaven, when all injuries shall be forgotten.